I0701007

Poisoned Soup for the Macabre, Depraved, and Insane:
Nostalgic Terrors

Poisoned Soup for the Macabre, Depraved, and Insane: Nostalgic Terrors

An Anthology Edited by

Wendy Dalrymple
and Grace R. Reynolds

Poisoned Soup for the Macabre, Depraved, and Insane: Nostalgic Terrors
Copyright 2025 © Brigids Gate Press

Individual works are copyright © 2025 by their respective authors and used by permission.

This book is a work of fiction. All of the characters, organizations, and events portrayed in these stories are either products of the author's imagination or are used fictitiously. Any resemblance to actual events or locales or persons, living or dead, is entirely coincidental.

All rights reserved. No part of this publication may be reproduced in any form or by any means without the express written permission of the publisher, except in the case of brief excerpts in critical reviews or articles. Nor can this publication be used in any manner for the purposes of AI data scraping and training.

No AI has been involved in the production of this book.

Edited by: Wendy Dalrymple and Grace R. Reynolds

Formatted by: Stephanie Ellis

Cover illustration by: Alison Flannery

First Edition: December 2025

ISBN (paperback): 978-1-963355-45-1
ISBN (ebook): 978-1-963355-44-4
Library of Congress Control Number:

BRIGIDS GATE PRESS
Overland Park, Kansas
www.brigidsgatepress.com

Printed in the United States of America

To those who find comfort in the dark

CONTENTS

A Note from the Editors:

Wendy Dalrymple

I am a nostalgic person at heart. I know that my proclivity for nostalgia comes from a place of privilege; I was fortunate enough to have a happy childhood thanks to wonderful parents, family, and friends. I often look back on my childhood through rose-colored glasses, and find myself wandering back to the things that I enjoyed then. I was a happy child, but I was also a frightened child; *everything* scared me: from the shadows on the wall to deep, dark, open water and stranger danger. So it was likely a surprise to my parents that their soft, overly sensitive little girl leaned so hard into horror.

When Grace approached me with the idea of compiling this anthology, I jumped at the opportunity. I am a nostalgic person, but I am also a nosey person, and I love discovering the backgrounds of my favorite authors, where they get their inspiration from, and why they write their specific genres. It's heartwarming for me to connect with another author and see that we had similar first brushes with horror, that we are all part of The Midnight Society in our own way, or that we all stayed up late watching horror movies or reading books that we weren't supposed to. I like to think that maybe some of us were all watching those same old TV shows at the same time; that in some lost timeline, we were all basking in the glow of a spooky VHS tape in tandem, or that we all picked up the same scary paperback from the Scholastic book fair when we were eight years old.

Horror has taught me that I am not alone, and that I can face the things that frighten me the most. Within these pages, my fellow authors have graciously shared their own first brushes with horror, and why they love the genre. So many of these authors were inspired by the same things that I was as a young horror author, and as you read along, I hope you find a few poems, drabbles, stories, and nonfiction pieces that resonate with you as well.

Thanks for coming along with us on this discovery of the macabre, depraved and insane.

Soups on!

Wendy Dalrymple

April 7, 2025, Florida, USA

A Note from the Editors:

Grace R. Reynolds

Severed toes. Resurrected cuts of meat. Amid reruns of *M*A*S*H (1972)*, *Lake Placid (1999)*, and *Poltergeist (1982)*, these images from core childhood memories of mine sound absolutely deranged when mentioned out of context. And yet, somehow, I know this anthology's readers will understand the nostalgia television and cinema such as these stir for someone like me.

You see, my father was an aircraft maintenance technician who worked the night shift for U.S. Airways, a company, like so many, that has since ceased to exist. A 'Constant Reader' in his own right, my dad was almost always the parent who would be home waiting for me after school, sometimes asleep in his chair, with at least one of these playing on the television. War comedy, monsters, and ghosts became the background noise to a childhood supplemented by the likes of *Goosebumps*, *Are You Afraid of The Dark? (1990)*, *Bunnicula*, and a cowardly dog in the middle of nowhere whose name, ironically, was Courage.

I met Wendy in the fall of 2023 in Richmond, Virginia, at an event called Halloween Hangover, where horror authors and readers alike came together to celebrate the strange, macabre, and downright terrifying world of horror literature. Together, we roamed the cobblestone pathways of the Edgar Allan Poe museum, past lines of graveyard-ivy in the enchanted garden, and communed with the black cats who greeted and guarded the museum's visitors. It was, to say, a delightful and spooky weekend. I cannot think of a better author to have coedited this anthology with!

Our desires for this anthology are three-fold: to celebrate, understand, and pull at the threads that bind this community together; a community that is so wonderfully ghoulish and full of heart. It is a shared love for this genre, in all its mediums, that brings us together in the first place, and it is our differences that make us stronger in a world that increasingly tells us to turn away from that which is horrific and gruesome. There is truth to be found in the world of horror. There is also love and hope too.

Thank you to our authors for sharing with us your words, first experiences, and that which drew you to the genre you hold dear. Thank you to our publishers, Heather and Steve of Brigids Gate Press, for seeing this project through and for your invaluable guidance. Thank you to our readers for picking up this book with an empty stomach, hungry for connection, ready to devour what follows in this anthology's pages.

We know you've been starving.

Grace R. Reynolds

April 7, 2025, Maryland, USA

INTRODUCTION

BY CHRISTI NOGLE

On your very first sleepover, you find that the family, headed by the preacher at your church school, has a chapel in their basement. Not a daylight basement, either. After refreshments (the soda in tiny Dixie cups, ice cream sliced into rectangles instead of scooped—who does that?), you are lured into a claustrophobic space with the family and the other sleepover invitees. You sit in half-length pews to worship and pray and then return to the rec room part of the basement to prepare for the movie. As you arrange the new sleeping bag purchased for this event, slippery pink nylon on the outside and baby blue flannel inside, you realize how uncomfortable you are and wish you could call your mother.

Their mother, cinched into a form-fitting church dress even at home, even on the weekend, helps with the VHS player and then she, along with the preacher and their younger children, heads upstairs, turning off the overhead light and then (*oh, please, no*) the stairwell light as they go.

The darkness is frightening in itself, but then the movie begins. What is this abomination, so entirely at odds with this family's aesthetic? Was it a mistake that they put it on? Maybe even a test? No one else is getting up or rebuking Satan and so you sit dead still and watch, knowing this kind of thing would be beyond taboo in your own home. You are rapt.

Does it scare you for weeks afterward? Do you find yourself afraid to look in mirrors in case you see someone else's face reflected? Some dead girl's face will appear instead of your own, the glass will crack, and you will lose whatever handle you pretend to have on reality. On your identity. Young as you are, you are still finding out what is real, what you believe, who you are, and maybe this movie will change things in some profound but indefinable way. Of course it will.

At home, lying on the carpet before the staticky screen of a console TV, you watch bucolic scenes give way to inverted and solarized images. You shiver as the voice-over intones, "Man lives in the sunlit world of what he believes to be reality. But, there is, unseen by most, an underworld, a place that is just as real, but not as brightly lit, a dark side." Even today, if you pull up *Tales from the Darkside* on YouTube, you'll get that shiver.

And what's the first book that scares you? Maybe ordered out of a Scholastic Book catalog, found at the library, loaned to you from an older sibling or parent, sneaked off of someone's shelves when they aren't looking, or bought (or lifted) from Waldenbooks at the mall. Is the cover seared into your memory, and do you recall where you were the first time you read it? Out on the weedy back lawn, maybe, lying on a towel in your swimsuit, goosebumped in the summer heat by what's happening on those pages.

Remember going into a Blockbuster, or better yet, a mom-and-pop rental store, poring over lurid horror posters and covers. Do you feel like the monsters and specters look out at you, call to you? They need something from you, just as you need something from them. Over a lifetime, your romance with them might bring nightmares and sleepless nights, a sense of wonder and curiosity, a sense of belonging, and more. Seeing them for the first time then and remembering them now, it's like two mirrors facing each other, reflecting infinite versions of yourself and those things you're drawn to and dread.

Though scenes such as the basement viewing and video store are common, they're not universal. Maybe you grew up earlier, or later, or in a place with different points of access to horror. You accessed it somehow, I think, or you would not be reading *Poisoned Soup for the Macabre, Depraved, and Insane: An Anthology of Nostalgic Terrors.*

In this fantastic book, Wendy Dalrymple and Grace R. Reynolds have brought together fifty-one works of poetry, nonfiction, and fiction that will sometimes resonate with your own experiences, other times surprise you, broaden your view, or send you searching for new-to-you gems. Contributors come from a diverse range of cultures, countries, and generations. You'll find happy families and unhappy families here, creepy kids and creeped-out kids, and a spectrum of horror from relatively cozy to intensely disquieting.

Though the pieces are varied, a few common threads run through this book:

Acceptance: accepting ourselves and our pasts, coming to terms with darkness, death, and troublesome desires.

The tension between otherness and connection:

As horror people, we find a bond to one another heightened by rejection we sometimes feel outside the community.

The courage to seek truth, even when it is frightening or painful. When we find ourselves afraid, or upset, or worried, many of us are told that nothing is wrong, that there's nothing to cry about. Horror media shows that something bad can and will happen. Though that may be terrifying, it feels validating because it feels true. Maybe horrors can't always be overcome or even fought, but they can at least be acknowledged.

Freedom, as well. Many of the young characters here, as in "kids on bikes" nostalgic horror tales, are unsupervised, autonomous, and as capable of dealing with the unknown as any adult. (And there might even be some kids on bikes in this book, though not exactly the kids you expect to meet.)

Finally, and most emphatically, running through every piece is a passion for horror and deep appreciation for influential stories, films, movies, shows, and books. These writers love their genre and are paying tribute to it over and over again. I hope that, when one of these short works pique your interest, you'll seek out the writer's other work—and keep an eye out for what they do in the future! They have so much to show you.

Christi Nogle

June 5, 2025, Idaho, USA

Gather Round the Fire: Oral Traditions, Mythology and Folktales

At our core, we are storytellers, weaving our hopes and fears into the skeins of our lives. We create rich tapestries, continuing the age-old tradition of passing down ancestral knowledge to preserve our heritage, culture, and family histories to transcend the new age. We all are haunted, by monsters, demons, and ghosts too. Listen to them—what is it they have to say?

Los fantasmas en Su Boca

by Richard Leis

I remember little of the Spanish I learned in her honor,
can include with online help only a little here, like
the weekends we visited la casita amarilla de mi bisabuela

in southeast Portland, donde ella hugged her unhappy white
"hijitos" y nuestra madre she adored, and fed us warm tortillas,
beans, and stories. One day, when I had a headache

she put me to bed in her dark bedroom. I could not sleep
and suffered there until los fantasmas emerged from
the closet to whirl like tornadoes and threaten me

with their pale mischief and unfathomable loneliness.
They darted alrededor mi cabeza y se rieron. I hid under the covers
and shook until my shouting brought her to me. La luz

could not expel their wispy harms, so she snatched them
con sus dientes and chewed, repelling their ancient stain.
Or mine? Her absence has not prepared me for living

outside the shape of those who used to be among
the living. Her family in my family tree. Her language.
I gaze up seguro y amado while she is devoured.

THE *HWYL* OF HORROR

ESSAY BY CATHERINE MCCARTHY

Hwyl, a word we use in Wales to mean *from the heart*. Hwyl is a stirring sensation of fervor and emotion, one that rouses passion. Hwyl is a fitting word through which to express what the horror genre means to me, because horror is part of who I am. It always has been, for the following reasons …

How can a child proclaim to be both happy and solemn, sociable but preferring one's own company, innocent and yet more aware of life's tribulations than they should be? I don't rightly know, but I do know I was that child, and I believe being that child made me more empathetic and aware of the "other" than most of my peers.

I cannot remember a time when I wasn't in touch with my dark side. From a young age I was keenly aware of illness, grief, death, and the powerful consequences such states have on us humans. Such personality traits stemmed from my mother, a wonderful woman who I miss to this day.

Her father, and later her brother and nephew, were sextons of the local church, an ancient building dating from the thirteenth century.

The graveyard in which they worked included the grave of her young brother, so my grandfather was reminded of his son's death on a daily basis. No maudlin, though, my grandfather would speak of the son he had lost as if he were still with him. I guess in a way he was.

I will never forget the story of how her brother died. Maybe I was too young to be told such a story, but my mother hid little from me. Named Hubert, and known affectionately as Hubie, he died of pneumonia, aged just three. My grandmother kept a jar of pennies on the kitchen shelf, savings for a rainy day, and Hubie loved to play with the pennies. On the night he died he asked for the jar of pennies, hugging it close while my grandmother nursed him. He spoke repeatedly of a woman in the corner of the room, a woman no one else could see, and just before he died he dropped the jar of pennies and spoke one word before taking his last breath: "Finished."

Strangely enough, my uncle who worked at the same church also had a son who died at the age of three, this time from a brain tumor, so he, too, spent the rest of his working life in the presence of his son's grave. I never met anyone who handled death the way my grandfather and uncle did, and I never have since.

I guess this is what I mean when I say I grew up in the realms of horror, despite a very happy childhood.

We were a very traditional family. My father worked while my mother kept house and looked after us. Every Friday night, my father would visit the local pub with my uncle, but before he went he would pop to the local shop and buy us sweets—a quarter pound of toffee rolls or sherbet lemons—then my mother, brother, and I would watch a movie.

My favorite movies were Hitchcock's *The Birds* and *Psycho*, and Robert Aldrich's black-and-white classic *Whatever Happened to Baby Jane?* with Bette Davis and Joan Crawford. Regardless of how many times I watched it, each time Joan Crawford's character took the silver cover off the dinner plate and discovered her sister had served the pet budgie for dinner it made me reel. The fact that the character played by Joan Crawford was a paraplegic and therefore, to some degree, helpless, made the horror of the situation so much worse. I also remember finding the mental regression of Bette Davis's character at the end of the film horrific, the psychological horror of her losing her mind simply terrifying.

Other favorites growing up were the classics *Night of the Hunter* and *The Wicker Man* starring Edward Woodward. My brother would hold a cushion to his face during the scary bits, but I never flinched, no matter how scared I was.

My choice of reading material was darkly classic too. Books such as *Jane Eyre* and *Wuthering Heights* were among my favorites. This is the kind of horror I mostly choose to write—the Gothic, characters with a twisted psychology, family secrets ripe for unveiling. These elements can be found in my novellas *Immortelle* and *Mosaic* as well as in my novel *A Moonlit Path of Madness*.

From a young age I adored portal fiction, especially if the stories had a dark edge. This love of portal fiction inspired my first ever collection,

Door and other twisted tales as well as my most recent novella, *The House at the End of Lacelean Street.*

I met my husband while we were still at school. I was fourteen and he was sixteen when we went on our first date. His love of what might be considered more pulp horror introduced me to works such as Herbert's *The Rats* and *The Fog,* King's *Cujo* and Masterton's *The Manitou,* all of which opened my mind to a different kind of horror fiction.

Those were the days when no one worried if you were underage at the cinema. Going to the midnight movies to watch *The Exorcist* was easy as pie, then came movies such as *The Omen, Carrie,* and *An American Werewolf in London,* all of which became firm favorites.

So, folks, it's been a journey, a journey I'm still travelling. Nowadays I gain inspiration from all kinds of places—from the darkly rural countryside, centuries-old graveyards, ancient woodlands as well as images and stories I come across during the course of everyday life.

My story in this anthology was inspired by a news article I read recently about a Welsh photographer, one who photographs sites where women have been murdered and buried in shallow woodland graves. In the article[1] she talks about how much of them is still present and the traces they leave behind, not in a macabre sense, but in the changes in plant life and atmosphere of the place. I was astounded to learn that approximately one hundred and seventy women are murdered every year in the U.K., the majority of whom are killed by a husband or partner. Such dreadful statistics of femicide are all too real, all too tangible.

From child to middle age, my thirst for the dark has never diminished. I doubt it ever will.

Yours,

Catherine McCarthy

---

[1] Nicola Bryan, "Murdered Women Championed by Shallow Grave Photos," BBC News, August 18, 2024, https://www.bbc.co.uk/news/articles/c199glg43r8o.

FROM EARTHEN GRAVE TO FEATHERED WING

BY CATHERINE MCCARTHY

Her final breath laced the air with sorrow and sent the dormouse scurrying into the undergrowth. The old oak, beneath which the man proceeded to bury her in a few inches of soil, gathered the molecules of her death into its mothering arms and placed them in its crown for safekeeping. As her twisted limbs became one with its roots, the crow nesting in the highest branch bowed its black head in mourning.

As synapse after synapse fired its last signal, the woman was comforted by good memories: a frayed old sofa on which she ate buttered toast slathered in honey, the soft plumpness of her mother's arms that brought comfort regardless of her age, the rhythmic hiss and lull of waves as they broke on the pebbled shore of The Parrog.

In the seven minutes it took for her brain to accept the fact that her heart no longer beat, not once did she think of him.

Flora and fauna watched him leave, covering his tracks as best he could and taking the length of cord he had tied around her neck with him. The stink of his sweat remained as a witness, acrid and riddled with guilt. There was nothing any of them could do, not the oak or the crow or the mouse, except watch and wait, and hope that *The Other* would come soon.

***

It was the sound of the flute that pried the woman out of the blackness—a soft, sweet tune that belonged in the realm of the fae. To her right, an old oak beneath which lay an area of ground unlike the rest—smoother, less compact, as though the knitted blanket of moss and lichen had been raked by a giant's fingers. She looked upward toward the crown of the oak, saw it shudder as a sudden gust of wind plucked a few of its golden leaves and scattered them at her feet as an offering. *Autumn,* she thought, but the concept of what the word encompassed no longer dwelled in her mind, despite her attempts to locate it.

The music stopped, and the forest was shrouded in mist so she could not see more than a few feet ahead. Two steps forward, her feet fell silent on the carpet of leaves. Weightless.

A fallen tree barred her way, and perched atop it was a female form. The woman studied the creature, drinking in every detail. Hair a braid of ivy, held in place with a coil of bramble that bore juicy blackberries. Angular cheekbones, chiseled by a master carver. Pools of wisdom shone in dark eyes, and her slender frame was draped in a green gown. Green as the forest. Green as grass. All kinds of green. She sat with one leg stretched in front of her, as though the knee refused to bend, and propped at her side was a pair of crutches, the wooden kind from long ago.

In her hand she held a piccolo, and when she saw the woman watching she lifted it up and played, her full lips trembling as she blew. The melody summoned the woman to her side, so that they sat thigh to thigh, shoulder to shoulder, and when she had finished the creature passed the instrument to the woman and nodded.

"Play," she said.

"I can't," said the woman. "I don't know how."

"Ah, but you do," said The Other, with a gentle nudge.

So the woman put the piccolo to her bloodless lips and played a tune that heartened the birds of the forest to join in the chorus, until the twilit air was filled with a melancholic aura.

When she had finished, she placed the piccolo in a hollow part of the tree trunk and stared down at her feet, for the playing had unsettled her. She saw that her feet were bare, encrusted with dirt and swollen at the ankle.

"Am I dead?" she asked The Other. She toed a candlesnuff fungus, dislodging it from the earth as she awaited the reply, and the crow in the crown of the oak cawed loudly, for it already knew the answer.

"Dead, or somewhere else entirely?" asked The Other.

A second gust blew at the woman's feet, causing the carpet of leaves to rise and swirl in a clockwise spiral. She followed the motion with her gaze, and her mind calmed.

The Other's features gave way to sorrow. "So many like you," she said, caressing her own shoulder, and the woman saw that the shoulder was misshapen and wondered why.

"What do you mean?" she asked, her eyes narrowing with suspicion.

"Slain," said The Other. "By the very menfolk who were meant to protect them. Buried in makeshift graves and left to rot in the ground." She took the woman's hands in hers, though hers were warm and dry and knotted with spurs, while the woman's were cold as ice. "That is what they hope when they bury them—that the body will rot and there it will end."

On hearing these words, the woman pulled a hand from The Other's grasp and held it to her throat. No pulse or heat, instead a ridge of flesh where the cord had been. Cord that had refused to be satisfied until it had stolen her last breath. Why, then, was she not afraid?

"And where are they now?" she said, gazing around at the forest. "The women you speak of."

The Other stretched her arms above her head and yawned. "Forgive me," she said. "I am tired." Then she stood, placing her weight on one leg. She picked up one of the crutches and nestled it deep in her armpit, and with the free hand she pointed into the distance. "In answer to your question, they are here, there … everywhere."

The woman looked in the direction she pointed but saw nothing except the forest. "I cannot see them," she said.

"Ah, but you have not yet learned to read the signs," said The Other. "Come, let us walk."

The woman stood and handed The Other the second crutch.

"And the piccolo," said The Other. "I must not forget the piccolo, or how else might I call them?"

The two traversed the forest as day turned to dusk, the wildest creatures with secrets of their own following in their wake. The fox and the hare, the squirrel and the shrew. The thrush and the wren and, as the skies darkened, they were joined by the owl.

As they journeyed, The Other pointed out the signs.

"See," she said, pausing at a clump of red campion, the petals of which had closed for the day. "You'll not find it anywhere else in the forest. It's a sign, you see. And here—" she said, picking up a pallid, alien thing that the woman did not recognize. She placed it in the center of her palm and peered close. "Stag beetle pupa," she said. "If we were to dig, we would most likely find more. They suggest a burial in the soil, maybe animal, possibly human." She blew, and the empty casing took to the air where it spun like a whirligig before coming to land.

Dips in the soil, subtle mounds of earth, leaf piles and lichen, fungi and flora. The Other showed her the changes in the landscape, and the woman recognized it for what it was—a peaceful place. A place where torment, pain, and fear no longer existed.

They journeyed throughout the night until they had come full circle. They studied the fallen tree upon which they had rested, marveling at the fibrous roots that were no longer anchored to the ground and at the place where its back had broken, for now the woman saw it differently to before, for The Other had opened her eyes to death and sorrow.

"Do not despair for the tree," said The Other as she pointed toward the lightening sky. "See how its downfall has left a hole in the canopy? Now, sunlight can reach the forest floor, and in doing so, new seedlings and wildflowers long forgotten by this forest will be given a chance to thrive."

The woman considered her words and nodded, though her limbs had grown stiff and she could not remember a time when she had felt this spent.

The Other recognized her suffering and gestured for them to sit once more on the fallen tree.

Morning held the reins now, and the sun granted the forest a gentle hint of warmth. A Holly Blue butterfly settled on the woman's thigh, its curious antennae twitching.

"So delicate," the woman said. "Its silver wings are almost transparent."

The Other smiled, and the woman saw that in place of teeth her gums were barbed with rose thorns.

"It is here because of death," The Other said. "For it feeds on the juice of rotting fruit and carrion."

The woman flinched, and the Holly Blue took flight.

"You see," said The Other. "Nothing ever truly dies."

They sat in silence for a long while, each alone with their thoughts.

"What about me?" the woman asked. "Where am I now?"

The Other took a deep breath, and let it out slowly. "You are here, beside me," she said, then she pointed toward the feet of the old oak, and the crow on its bough fell still. "And you are there too."

And the woman remembered the smoothness of the soil beneath the tree. She remembered how its mossy blanket had been stripped away. She peered at the flattened soil beneath the tree and saw that while she had walked the forest the blanket had been replaced by one of golden leaves and weighted down with acorns. A squirrel nibbled a nut from its paws and watched her with almond eyes that shone like glass.

And the woman understood that she was both here, and there. She felt no fear, no sadness or remorse, only immense fatigue.

The Other stood, and the shape at her shoulder shifted, unfurling into a great wing, and then another, until she no longer found it necessary to depend on the crutches for the wings bore her weight.

Never before had the woman seen such wings, for they were vast and all the colors of the rainbow. Brunette and blonde, black and grey and silver white. Now and then a flash of cobalt, raspberry pink or lavender blue. The woman stroked the feathered wings with the tip of her finger, noting the straightness of each spine and the warmth that transferred to her cold flesh.

The Other said nothing. Instead she embraced the woman's touch.

"Where did you find them?" the woman asked. Her voice faltered, and she frowned. "Are you an angel?"

"I am of the forest, not the heavens," said The Other, "but you can call me whatever you want." Her wings beat slowly, flaunting their myriad colors in the sunlight. "It's like this," she said. "These feathers are your sisters, for each one has suffered a similar fate to you. Each has her own shade, and a spine far stronger than mine. We bear each other's burdens, and our togetherness makes us strong."

The woman frowned, for she was puzzled.

"See here," said The Other, pointing at a small space in the primary wing. "It can be yours if you want it."

The woman considered The Other's offer. How would she fit between the honey brown and copper red? She reached around to touch her own spine, and saw that her wrist faced the wrong way. The flesh mottled purple and the fingers so puffy that the gold band on the fourth finger dug a deep channel. With all her might she tugged at the ring, and in time it relinquished its grip. She left The Other and approached the old oak, setting the ring down on the ground beneath which her body was buried. Perhaps someone would find it, perhaps not. It no longer mattered.

Returning to The Other's side, she fingered the gap in the wing. "I accept," she said.

The old oak, the crow, and all the creatures of the forest sighed. And the wind claimed the sigh for itself, for it knew that such things belonged to the land of dreams.

Grotte De La Folie

Essay by Basil Inspiratie

Kahf Ajnoon, known to the world by its French name Grotte de la Folie, meaning "the cave of madness," is a small mountain in the south of Libya, located about 40 kilometers from the city of Ghat. The cave Kahf Ajnoon gained its French name because of a mistranslation, for in the Arabic language the word madness has the same letters as the plural of djinn.

I first learned about Grotte de La Folie from my mother, when she had shown me a picture of it. An old, grainy black-and-white photo, on it was my grandfather, behind him a rocky mountain. The thing that caught my eye was how the mountain looked. Almost half of it formed into this fortress-like structure.

I asked my mother if Grandpa had a castle, whose answer has stuck with me to this day. She said that "it wasn't a place for people." Undeterred, I pestered her about it the next day and her answer remained the same: "you can ask Grandpa when you see him."

The next time we visited my grandparents I blew past all my aunts and cousins, making a beeline to the kitchen, where my grandfather usually was. He was sitting at the kitchen table, the Quran in front of him. I climbed up on the chair next to him, photo in hand, and waited for him to finish reciting the verses.

I sprang up in excitement as he finally turned to me, a flurry of questions spilling from my mouth as I showed him the photo. He listened, with a smile, waiting for me to pause before beginning the story of his time in the south.

I forget why he had travelled there exactly; something to do with friends he had made during his time in Benghazi. Once he was there, though, he barely spent any time under a roof, camping most days.

The group's guide, a local Tuareg man, seemed to have a permanent smile on his face. He had driven my grandfather's group around many of the sights, excitedly sharing all that he knew about the area, whether it was personal experience or local legend.

One day during a drive through the Sahara the group grew bored, with nothing to pass the time. Back then, no radio channel reached that far south and while the guide did own a car (a rare thing back in those days) its AC didn't work. The blistering sun was taking its toll on them.

It was then that over the horizon one of them spotted it; a giant looming structure with nothing but sand dunes and desert surrounding it for miles. Asking the guide what it was, he cautioned them, saying it was better to stick to the plan and continue to Ghat. But the group didn't waver and, after a bit more grilling, the guide hesitantly told them what he knew.

According to the Tuareg, it was the fortress of the djinn; beings made of smokeless fire, invisible to the naked eye. They convened here to discuss their affairs. A local legend spoke of a young man who would spend his time near the mountain for its quiet and tranquil nature. Each passing day the young man would get closer and closer, ignoring the warnings of his elders, until one day he had vanished. They scoured the desert searching for him for days, but it was as if he never existed.

The group bustled with excitement, pushing the guide to park at the side of the dirt path. They posed for pictures and searched the area for a path up the mountain. My grandfather stayed behind with the guide so he wouldn't run off and leave them stranded.

The group didn't even make it a third of the way up before coming back. Weary and severely dehydrated, darkness began to set in so they decided to spend the night there and recuperate while my grandfather and the guide took charge of setting up the tents. After eating dinner, they all sat around the campfire for warmth, still not accustomed to the desert night's chill.

Discussing the day until they grew too tired to speak, they all crawled into their tents. My grandfather, curled up and shivering under his blanket, couldn't seem to fall asleep, tossing and turning in the cold until he heard a sound.

It was faint at first, far and hard to make out. A rhythmic thumping that resounded through the desert with each passing second. As the sound drew nearer it started to become more and more recognizable: horses galloping through the desert. Their whinnies echoed in the distance, and they were growing closer and closer, until the sound surrounded him right outside the tent.

My grandfather bolted from under the blanket, stumbling outside. The sound fading as soon as his eyes adjusted to the darkness. He looked around him and saw the guide hurriedly taking down the tents, while the rest of their group stood frozen like deer in headlights. The guide barked instructions at them to get their things, sparking a sense of panic through the camp.

The group frantically leaped into the car, and as the guide drove off the sound returned: a chorus of ethereal hooves thudding against the distant ground.

It wasn't until an hour or so later, when they finally reached Ghat, that the sound had stopped. The group hardly talked about it during the rest of the trip, quietly agreeing to take a longer route home.

I wanted to know more about it, but couldn't bring myself to ask my grandfather. Even if I did, I'm sure he wouldn't speak about it further. For the next few years, whenever I misbehaved my mother would scare me by saying she'd leave me at the cave. Now, as an adult, I can tell you one thing about Kahf Ajnoon, the Grotte de la Folie.

Avoid it.

LA GRINGA LLORONA

BY ROBERTO COFRESÍ HOPGOOD

She's wrapped in rags. Her bare feet, hands, and face are caked with mud and dirt. Her eyes are black wells surrounded by the tangled clouds of her white hair.

The flames burst from the top of the steel drum for her eyes only. Behind the fire, she can see the colored lights of fireworks exploding against the moonless Mexico City night.

How long has she been by this fire?

The air is thick with the sulfuric smell and smoke of a million firecrackers. The new millennium has arrived. People dance and kiss on the streets. Kids light sparklers on balconies. Everyone celebrates.

A man puts a paper bag on the ground near her.

"Para usted," he says and steps away, head down, without turning his back.

She watches him fade away into the smoke and darkness, shakes her head like a cat might, and wraps her once colorful sarape tighter around her. Still crouching, she opens the bag. A half empty bottle of mezcal and a bread roll. She opens the bottle and takes a swig, feels the liquor go down, but it doesn't warm her.

She stares at the fire, sees the red-and-blue flames flicker in the night. She remembers being warm but doubts she'll ever be warm again.

A group of young teens approach her. She doesn't turn around, but she can feel them. She can feel their heat, smell their sweat, sense their fear. They get closer with one careful step after another. It's like they're playing Red Light, Green Light. They take a step and stop to see if she turns, egging each other on, testing their own limits.

Will she turn them to stone with her stare? Will she enslave them to work in the pits of Hell? Will she hypnotize them into forgetting everything they hold dear? Will she possess them and eat them alive from the inside? Or are those all fake stories their parents tell them about La Gringa Llorona?

What does she have to cry about anyway? She's just some old American woman.

She can feel them inching closer. They want to touch her, but do they dare? They want to be able to tell their friends, "I wasn't afraid of La Gringa Llorona."

How close will they get? And what will she do if they dare to touch her?

She doesn't want to think about it. She wants to be left alone next to the fire. Wrapped in her sarape.

She used to live in the United States. She used to be from a place. She used to have people. Now she's a crying specter.

A couple of feet from her and the teens can't take it anymore.

All at once they yell and throw what they have at her: an empty soda can, some used food wrappers, a popsicle stick. No rocks this time.

They all back away to what they consider a safe distance. All but one.

"Cheo!" His friends call him, now nervous for him, but he's not backing away. He's in position to take another step.

Without turning, she can feel his warm breath tangled in her hair. She can smell his body trembling a step behind her. She can hear him thinking, trying to convince himself to take another step.

He does.

She does not turn around. Not yet. The punishment is best when doled out at the right time. Any moment now, he's going to try to touch her.

Hot tears from her eyes burn a track through the mud on her face.

He extends a hand and touches her shoulder.

She wails and turns toward Cheo. Their eyes meet and he sees the infinity of her horror. He sees centuries of pain; holes like mine shafts into her soul. He gets sucked into them going deeper and deeper until he arrives at the bottom of the frozen hell she has inside. Cheo sees generations of violent men, old men, young men: all killing, raping, pillaging. He sees poor men, rich men, sick men destroying everything around them with bats, guns, knives, and ancient weapons long forgotten. An old man grabs him by the arm, his face and body covered in a crisscross pattern of scars and wrinkles. The old man puts his mouth onto Cheo's mouth and breathes fire into his lungs.

Cheo screams.

La Gringa Llorona closes her eyes and turns back toward the fire.

Cheo falls backwards. He looks around, but his friends are gone. Scattered into their lives.

He turns towards La Gringa Llorona but she is gone, too, vanished. A cold breeze blows from Columbus Avenue. The sidewalk is covered with dirty snow. Fireworks explode over the Manhattan skyline. It's a new century, but Cheo is still trying to understand what happened. His memory of it does not seem right. He tastes the old man's ashes in his mouth, the sulfur burning his nostrils. Cheo's hair is long around him. His beard touches the floor. He wraps his sarape tight, but he is still cold.

He leans back against the glass door of the glass building trying to feel some of the heat from the inside. He wishes he was sitting by a fire.

A man in a long leather coat walks by him. Without looking at Cheo, the man throws some coins on the sidewalk.

CHI-CHI MAN

ESSAY BY C.L. PRATER

Bigfoot wasn't the name we used. On the Rosebud Reservation in South Dakota, our version of the hairy man was Chi-Chi Man. We pronounced it "chee-chee" or "gee-gee." As Lakota was an oral language, I never saw it written.

We teased, making up scary stories of him as we played in the long endless rays of summer. When leaves began to fall and our big sky turned pink then purple while we walked the dirt roads home from school, our talk turned serious, dark as our uncovered windows.

We huddled together during fourth grade recess, trying to break the wind that ballooned our skirts. Our girlish conversation jumped from an older boy who swore X-ray glasses really *did* see through clothes, to Chi-Chi Man sightings. A cousin's cousin saw one running through trees at the edge of Chases Woman Lake. Another heard of one near Ghost Hawk Park.

"I got up to use the bathroom last night," Donna interrupted. We turned, ears attuned. Donna lived in the school dormitory and never said much. "I saw a green light through the hallway window. I went close. Chi-Chi Man was staring at me."

No one doubted her.

In sixth grade, too old for goofy costumes and babyish trick-or-treating, Carol and I devised something spookier. We would leave from my house on the far edge of town and walk the mile and a half to her sister's home in the country. It was a delicious, heart-thumping plan on the scariest night of the year.

For safety, we would carry a flashlight. For fun, we would each have a leg of pantyhose stuffed in our pocket. When we got to her sister's house, we would slide the hose over our faces and knock.

The plan was vetoed. Carol's mother had heard her coworkers talk about missing girls and Chi-Chi Man sightings. My disappointment had an outer rim of relief. Carol's mom was the first adult in my world to acknowledge Chi-Chi Man might actually exist.

My father chuckled over the sightings. He believed myths like these were created long ago to keep children from wandering. He still did not become a believer, even after our mother screamed at a face that flashed past our back bedroom window.

My six-foot-two dad went running outside. A punch came out of nowhere. He was lucky. His disbelief cost him only a loose front tooth.

Cattle mutilations soon made the news. Rustlers and rattlesnakes, even the escaped convict that barricaded himself into Kim's ranch house seemed trivial in comparison to a flesh-eating ritualistic creature. I wondered if Chi-Chi Man had family members.

I began a ritual of my own, closing curtains and pulling down roller shades at dusk. It was protection against seeing those dashboard green eyes. And yet we still played in the frosty air after dark, close to the yard light, away from the rows of dark trees that bordered our yard.

Beyond our trees was open pasture, rolling hills and a decaying farmhouse. A pack of wild dogs, known to shelter there, would roam the town at night. On several occasions, pets left outside were found dead.

After a time, the dog sightings ended. Speculation was that someone or something had "taken care" of the dogs. In my mind, Chi-Chi Man had topped their food chain.

I had a recurring dream in those years of playing hide-and-seek with my friends all night long. It was a good dream or at least started as one. The only curious difference was that our mothers, who in real life called us in before bedtime, let us keep playing. I always woke before the dream ended.

Dreams of falling became our new topic at school. Bonnie said that if you actually hit the ground, you would die. Darla said if you have a bad dream that ends before you wake, it really happens. I began to worry.

The dream came again, more real than before. It was exhilarating, playing in the dark. I was fearless. I sat joyful, silent behind hefty trunks, peering strategically between branches, watching for a break to run out of the shadows. I made it to our back door every time. I was always safe.

As light began to show on the horizon, I confidently burst through the trees once more at full speed. As I got closer, there were no kids, no calling mothers, only me. My veins filled with slow motion. My legs would not pump. I forced my head to turn.

Chi-Chi Man was it.

THE HEADLESS QUEEN

BY NGÔ BÌNH ANH KHOA

A queen visited a slumbering man, holding a baby swaddled in golden cloth. Only there was nothing above her neck, save a dripping pool of red. Yet she spoke, her voice echoing in the foggy, staticky air. She floated forward, pleading incessantly. Her accuser screamed himself awake, and so did the viewers, broken out of their trance.

The Headless Queen, a Vietnamese play recorded on an innocent, unlabeled VHS tape, left my childish self haunted by the horrors of the beyond, planting a seed within my mindscape that blossomed into a grotesque flower, nurtured by the shadows of the macabre.

THE PHANTOM OF YOUTH: FOUNDATIONAL HORRORS

As children, we sought security in those we loved and trusted when so much around us made us feel powerless or uncertain. We came of age in turbulent times only to find monsters that didn't just exist in the back of our closets, underneath our beds, or at the bottom of the basement stairs. Horror served as a cornerstone for us, reminding us more than shadows lurked in the dark: our bravery did too.

Traps

by Kate Falvey

I.

She tucked me into my four-poster bed
with an immaculately weary, singsong sigh.

My little room was gussied up with red curtains
she had sewn, fringed with white pom-poms I liked

to flick or watch shiver slightly in the chill window-leaks
and make up stories about the pom-pom town

where every fuzzy ball was a head hanging on by a thread,
all lining up to defend against the scissor-beaked bird

who would make heads roll if I didn't say the spell.
The spell said Scissor Bird, Scissor Bird, Sleep is the word.

Go eat worms. Or sometimes, when she plugged in the scissors
by day and let me hold the squat red torso and beak through the

heart shapes on pale red construction paper, I would become
the Scissor Bird at night and find pom-pom heads on the sill

when I woke to sugared cinnamon toast, ice-box-frosty milk,
and weary, honeyed patience.

II.

I told her that in the night I opened a secret invisible
trap door that led to mazy tunnels that snaked from Flushing

to the Bronx. I'd spiral down the metal stairs into
a wet landscape of gray stone and greening metal, and

I'd find my way to Grandma's kitchen with the sauce
pot rattling, the laundry strung between buildings,

and the cats in the alley yowling over scraps as they
clanked metal garbage can lids and dodged old boots

flung at them by thick-voiced men growling in Italian.
Grandma expected me, and let me dip the bread in the sauce

even though it was night. Then she unfolded the cot and I sunk
into the scratchy covers while streetlights yellowed the air

and the lion-faced ceiling lamp stuck light bulbs at me like
bulbous eyes and tongue. A doll shaped like me was in my

bed in Queens, I told her, and she never knew the difference.

In Creature We Trust: All Others Pay Cash

Essay by Robert P. Ottone

Christmas, 1986.

Two-year-old Robert stepped carefully down the black-and-white tiled stairs. They were cold under his feet. Always were. He'd barely slept that night. After a Christmas Eve at his aunt's house out east, Robert had been tired, sure, but more importantly, he wanted to be home, because if he wasn't home, Santa might not come.

It was little kid logic, sure, but nevertheless, when Robert heard the jingle bells outside his window a sleepless hour after getting tucked into bed by his dad and read *The Night Before Christmas*, he was happy he'd made it home in time. Christmas was serious business, after all. After Halloween, it was Robert's favorite. Even at two years old, Robert knew that under the tree that morning would be multicolored delight, that somehow the candy-colored boxes would contain his obsessions for the year to come.

Halfway down the steps, the boy picked up the aroma of fried bread dough. "Guinea pancakes," his mother, Joanne, always called them, never intending to be offensive with the Italian slur, since her grandparents were off-the-boat and her parents were first-generation to America. It's just what her grandparents called them, and by extension, what she called them too.

Robert, wearing his *Gremlins* T-shirt, a pair of tighty-whitey underpants and dragging his yellow satin baby blanket behind him, passed the family room and snuck a peek at the Douglas fir propped up in the corner. A veritable ocean of red, gold, green, blue and yellow-wrapped magic lay beneath the tree. He felt a hitch in his chest knowing he had to wait for the rest of his family to wake up before diving into the swell headfirst.

"Merry Christmas, Mommy," the boy said, pulling a chair away from the kitchen table and climbing up. He plopped down and yawned.

"Merry Christmas," she said, wrapped in her purple robe. She walked over and hugged him, planting a kiss on his forehead. "Hungry?"

"Yeah," he said, turning and trying to get a look into the family room. He could see a few presents sticking out through the entry from the dining room, and again, he felt that hitch of excitement in his chest. He wrapped his baby blanket around him and turned his attention to the glass sliding door, toward the pool area. A light snow had come down overnight. Not enough to play in, but just enough to give the appearance of a white Christmas on Long Island.

"When your father comes down," Mom began. "Maybe he'll let you open one before your brother and sister wake up."

"Okay." The boy smiled.

The wait was excruciating.

***

"This is the last year we do these bubble lights," Dad muttered, as Robert stood nearby, now wearing sweatpants and socks. Bob Ottone, the patriarch of the family, turned to Robert. "Your mother and these damned things. Look, they don't even work."

Robert giggled and watched as his dad struggled to force the bulbs upright, only to watch them twist on the thin green cable and go upside down again.

"That's it," Dad said, rising off his knee. "I give up."

"I can fix them," Robert said.

"No, no," Dad said. "I think I hear your brother, it's time to open presents."

"Wait until he comes down!" Mom shouted from the kitchen. She was busying herself with the endless wave of hors d'oeuvres she'd prepared for the multitude of guests they'd be receiving throughout the day. Neighbors. Family friends. Aunts and uncles from out of town. Grandparents. Robert especially looked forward to the arrival of his dad's friends, who always made him laugh, were altogether too loud, sometimes vulgar, and always the most fun.

Later in life, Robert would refer to his father's friends as his "cronies," then appropriate the term for his own best friends.

"Feh!" Dad said, waving his wife's words away as though they were a gnat. He leaned down and grabbed one brightly wrapped present and handed it to his youngest son. "Here. Don't let her see."

Robert smiled and walked out of his mom's view, putting the tree between himself and her. He tore into the present, quickly revealing what lay underneath. Something that he wouldn't realize at the time would make such an impact on his life.

In his hands was a Remco Universal Monsters action figure—*The Creature From the Black Lagoon.*

Robert's eyes went wide and he looked up at his father. "Creature From the Black-y a la Goon!"

He'd seen the movie play on television, watching it with his parents, and recognized the Creature immediately. Though he couldn't quite say the name correctly, the glow-in-the-dark plastic nightmare in the blister pack before him held so much significance. Robert had been Dracula for Halloween, twice. He loved the Universal Monsters dearly. But deep down, it was the Creature that meant the most to him.

"Bob, I said to wait!" Mom called from the kitchen.

"It's like she's got a sixth sense," Dad said, shaking his head. "He glows in the dark."

"Can I open him?" Robert asked, excitedly.

"Don't open anything," Mom called again.

Dad laughed. "God forbid we have any *fun* on Christmas morning, right? Come on, let's crack some walnuts, you can open him on the couch."

***

Looking back. Thirty-eight years have passed. My mom and dad not only gave us the best Christmas a kid could ask for, with amazing food, warmth, love, gifts and more, but—most importantly—they fostered a love of the things we showed interest in. Where my aunts and uncles would get me sports-related nonsense, my parents helped me become the monster kid at Timber Point Elementary School.

The following Halloween, in 1987, my mom and I built a haunted dollhouse to go with those Remco Universal Monsters.

We put it out every year for Halloween.

It's mine now.

With all the Universal Monsters to go with it.

Every time I look at it, I think of my parents. My mom, who worked a second job at a toy store that Christmas season in 1986 to make extra money. My dad, who spent long days teaching and running the Brentwood High School radio station.

They worked so hard to give us everything we wanted, and we wanted for nothing.

I'm a monster kid because of them.

IN THE DEEP END

BY ROBERT P. OTTONE

Bob didn't hear the creak of the chain-link gate to the pool area.

He didn't hear the slam of metal on metal as the gate locked automatically when it closed.

He certainly didn't hear the splash as his five-year-old plunged into the murky depths.

What he *did* hear was his son, Robert, scream as he broke above the surface of the pool. In a flash, he tore out the back door of the house, then through the gate into the backyard. He hadn't moved this fast since high school.

For a few breathless moments, Bob's mind raced. His youngest son might be gone. At the bottom of the twelve-foot-deep end, lungs filled with water, eyes wide with terror. The swimming lessons he'd paid for would mean nothing in the face of panic.

By the time he reached the pool area, he watched as his oldest son, Eddie, leapt over the chain-link fence to the pool area in one swift motion. He'd been in the garage, blasting The Hooters' *Nervous Night* album over and over while assembling his new hockey net. The most athletic of his three kids, Eddie dove without hesitation into the pool, emerging after a few heart-wrenching moments with the soaked and pale five-year-old in his arms.

Bob knelt over his youngest son as Eddie wiped leaves and gunk from the boy's face. Panic-stricken, Bob opened Robert's mouth to prepare to resuscitate him, but with a heavy cough and eruption of green-gray water from the boy's gullet, he knew his youngest was alright.

Robert looked at his older brother, then right into Bob's eyes.

"There was something in the water," Robert whispered, the sound of crickets chirping in the woods next to their home echoing softly as day was turning into evening.

***

Robert sat at the dining room table with his mom, drinking soda and eating a bowl of electric-green pistachio ice cream. She had one arm around him, holding him close.

"He was chasing a frog around the pool," Bob said to his oldest.

Eddie shook his head. "He said something pulled his ankle. Took his shoe right off."

Bob looked at his youngest's right ankle. The sock was torn, and there were definite scratches, four in total, jagged, but not deep. After assessing the child for further injury, they noticed the shoe was, in fact, missing. The sneakers, a tiny pair of Batman and Robin Velcro high tops, were no longer a dynamic duo.

"Maybe a raccoon?" Eddie asked. "Wouldn't be the first time the fuckers got into the pool."

There was a knock at the back door before it opened. Bob's in-laws, Mary and Edmund entered; arms laden with grocery bags. His wife had called them immediately after they pulled Robert from the pool and they rushed over. Bob was glad they lived so close, and were as helpful and supportive as they were.

"Hey, Grandma," Eddie said, walking over and taking the bags from his grandmother's arms.

She planted a smooch on his cheek, and lightly slapped him for good measure. "You weren't watching him? What were you thinking not watching the baby outside?"

"Grandma," Eddie began.

"It's not his fault," Bob said. "It was an accident, Robert was chasing a frog, and he went over the edge of the deep end."

"The deep end?" Grandpa asked. He looked through the pass-through from the kitchen into the dining room and waved to his daughter. "A frog?"

Bob nodded. "That's what he said."

Grandpa stared at the boy. "Mary, make some sandwiches. I'm gonna' talk to the boy."

***

Bob and Eddie sat on the porch staring at the pool area. Eddie sipped a can of Coke while Bob twiddled his thumbs. He didn't know what else to do as the night sky grew darker and his father-in-law talked to Robert in the den on the far side of the house.

Joanne emerged from the sliding door and stepped onto the porch. "They're still talking. Mom's cleaning up in the kitchen. She made two lasagnas for some reason."

"Does she think we don't have food or something?" Eddie asked, crushing the can.

"It's just her way." Joanne shrugged. "Old school Italian."

"What're they talking about in there?" Bob asked, straightening his glasses.

"Something about singing," Joanne said. "That's all I could hear before Dad found me snooping and closed the door."

"Singing?" Bob asked.

"We need to talk," Grandpa said, appearing as if from nowhere in the sliding doorway behind Joanne.

She yelped.

"Jesus, Pop," Joanne said. "Nearly gave me another heart attack. What do we need to talk about?"

"Not you," Grandpa said. "Me, Bob and Eddie."

"Alright," Bob said. "In the garage?"

Grandpa nodded. There was a grave look on his face the likes of which Bob had never seen. Edmund Clement wasn't a particularly serious man. Hardworking, yes, a good provider for his family, strong, smart, kind, but never overtly serious.

Bob watched as Grandpa took a pack of cigarettes out of his pocket, his hands shaking as he did so.

***

The three men stood in the garage. A halo of smoke lingered above Grandpa's head as he puffed on his second Marlboro Red.

"I was a little younger than Robert when it happened," Grandpa said. "So, a little over seventy years back."

"When *what* happened, Grandpa?" Eddie asked. He fumbled with a hockey stick nervously.

"My family didn't have much, but we had a small swimming hole at my family's home outside of Lisbon. This was before they came here to America."

Grandpa slid Eddie's weightlifting bench out from the corner and sat down.

"One day, I heard the sweetest sound I'd ever heard," Grandpa said. "And I saw rabbits and other little animals moving in the yard. Near the swimming hole." He smiled a moment and Bob realized how vividly his father-in-law was seeing the memory in his mind. "Something was singing. From *in* the water."

"Singing?" Bob asked.

"The baby boy today," Grandpa said. "He said he heard singing. That he saw a frog. That's what lured him toward the pool."

"*Lured* him?" Eddie asked.

Grandpa nodded. "The Coca. It's like a spirit. From the old country. Takes children. It tried to take me when I was a little boy. Now it's come for your son."

"This is nuts, Ed," Bob said. "He fell in the pool and he's making up a story because he thinks he's in trouble."

"The same story from when I was a boy? I've never told anyone other than Mary, and she sure as shit didn't tell your wife, so how would the baby know?" Grandpa said, his voice rising. He finished the cigarette and stamped it out with his boot.

"The Coca?" Eddie asked. "Like the drink?"

Grandpa smiled. "If that helps you." He rose and looked through one of the garage windows that overlooked the pool area. "She's in there. I believe Robert. You should too."

Bob rolled his eyes. "So what do we do? Add more chlorine? Drain the pool? Fill it in with cement?"

"We kill the bitch," Grandpa said.

***

Bob sat on the diving board, staring down into the inky blackness of the pool. Itinerant leaves and twigs floated on the surface, since it was only Memorial Day Weekend. Plenty of time to get the pool ready for the end of the school year, when the kids would have endless parties with their friends. Beside him was a hatchet. The last time he'd used it was to cut up some fallen tree limbs courtesy of Hurricane Gloria.

Grandpa waded in the shallow end, shirtless, tufts of gray curly chest hair flecked with water.

Eddie walked the perimeter, baseball bat in hand.

"If this thing is a spirit," Bob began. "Then how do we kill it?"

"*Spirit* means a lot of things, Bob," Grandpa said. "It's a physical being like any other, doesn't mean we can't kill it. Plenty of things in this world we don't know about."

A bubbling, gurgling sound caught Bob's attention. He thought at first it might have been the pool filter kicking on, but when he saw Robert's sneaker floating in the center of the deep end, he knew better.

"Ed," Bob whispered.

"I see it," Grandpa muttered.

"What do we do?" Eddie asked, his voice shaking.

Grandpa raised his hand to silence the teen, then drifted closer to the deep end. Bob watched as he pulled something from the back of his swim trunks. A knife?

"Careful," Bob whispered. He looked closer. In Grandpa's hand was a box cutter.

Grandpa drifted into the deep end of the pool, slowly kicking his way toward the floating sneaker. Bob rose from the diving board and fumbled for the hatchet, before gaining a grip and squeezing it tightly. He looked over at Eddie, who shifted left to right on his heels, baseball bat resting on his shoulders.

"Vai-te Coca, Vai-te Coca," Grandpa whispered, lightning bugs fluttering around above the surface of the pool. "Deixa o menino dormir."

"What're you saying?" Eddie asked.

Grandpa shook his head. He reached slowly for the sneaker, his legs kicking in the darkness below.

"Um soninho descansado," Grandpa whispered, his voice trembling lightly in the stillness of the night.

Bob's eyes went wide as the water erupted around his father-in-law. A great plume of fluid exploded skyward, the diving board tearing from the brick, and the ladders leading out of the deep end unmooring from the cement.

The flurry of action around the pool was alarming, as fast as the explosion happened, Bob turned his attention to the surface to find his father-in-law gone. Eddie, meanwhile, was backing away from something stalking toward him. Something lithe, something tall. Moving in a way that its arms swung side to side as if coursing through still water.

"Dad," Eddie stammered, backing away. He took a cursory swing of the baseball bat, swishing through the air between himself and the approaching creature.

Bob ran over quickly and swung hard, bringing the hatchet down into the creature's back. It screamed, an inhuman, albeit beautiful sound, perfectly pitched, the mix of an opera singer and pop star. The shriek was almost pleasing to the ear, and as the being spun around, Bob got a better look as the motion sensor light that had turned on during his run over to his oldest son bathed the creature in luminescence.

Feminine. Broad shoulders. Long legs and arms. Scales. Gills heaved, gulping fresh air. Bulbous, golden eyes twinkled in the light. A mouth of jagged, almost metallic-teeth snapped wildly.

This thing was built for the water.

It grasped madly for the hatchet dug in its back as Eddie began raining blows with the Louisville Slugger. Bob looked around for something else to use, since he was now weaponless. Grabbing the pool skimmer, he began jabbing the Coca in the gut, forcing her back toward Eddie, who continued his assault until finally, the bat splintered into a thousand pieces.

"Oh fuck," Eddie sighed.

The creature spun and swatted him away before diving back into the pool.

Bob rushed over to Eddie, who was in and out of consciousness, his head having slammed hard into the brick surrounding the pool.

Commotion drew Bob's attention to the deep end. Splashing. Manic, frenzied.

Grandpa emerged from the depths, the Coca wrenched in a headlock.

"Deixa o menino dormir! Um soninho descansado!" he screamed, stabbing her in the throat with the box cutter before dragging the blade slowly across her scaled throat.

Bob held Eddie as he completely lost consciousness, but kept his eyes on the deep end as the Coca's body went limp in his father-in-law's arms.

"Let the child have a quiet sleep," Grandpa whispered. The creature's glowing eyes went dark.

***

The long plastic tube that ran from the backyard to the front pumped every drop of water from the pool. Bob stood nearby, with Eddie, who sustained a concussion in the fight with the Coca. Green blood mingled with the water, and Grandpa watched as it disappeared down the nearby storm drain, cigarette dangling from his lips.

The cement mixer swirled, ready to fill in the pool.

Robert sat on the porch, playing with his superhero figures. Batman was fighting the Creature from the Black Lagoon. Robin and Superman were helping.

"Should be drained after dinner, then we can start filling it in," Grandpa said, walking over and taking a puff. "Bury the bitch in the cement for good."

Bob nodded.

"Thanks, Ed," Bob said, hugging his father-in-law.

"It's what grandpas do. Let's go eat, I'm starving," Grandpa said. He gave Eddie a light slap on the cheek. "Come on, dopey. Let's get some of Mary's manicotti in you."

Leave Coca. Leave Ccoca.
Go to the top of the roof.
Let the child have.
A quiet sleep.

How to Have a Funeral for Yourself

by Mir Rainbird

Brother and I, playing funerals again. Sometimes, there's violence first—a car crash, a kidnapping, a shooting, the helpless happenings we're taught to fear—and desperate cries for help. Sobbing first-aid attempts. Failure, grief. Other days we skip straight to death, weeping over each other's limp bodies. We take turns, mourner and mourned.

"Now I'm dead, and you cry."

He dies. I scour libraries for words about death, doom, despair. Demise, suggested by my mother, who tells me she used to lie under the sofa and pretend she was in her coffin. She doesn't ask what I'm searching for.

Miss Pumpkinhead

by Ivana Geček

It may seem crazy, but this whole thing started with a PEZ dispenser.

I received the candy one day in late September, back in the '90s. PEZ was all the craze back then: my six-year-old eyes went cartoonishly wide as my mom took the dispenser out of the grocery bag and plopped it on the kitchen counter. What was meant as a harmless Halloween trinket instantly became my obsession: I was inexplicably drawn to the little jack-o'-lantern that adorned the top of the plastic case, all beautifully orange and round and shiny. I ran my fingers against its smooth surface. Goose bumps prickled along my spine. Black, triangle-shaped eyes stared at me, and I stared right back at them, at the endless pits of dark. I was thrilled and terrified at the same time. I smiled, and matched its almost toothless grin.

I named the dispenser Miss Pumpkinhead.

I spent all of my time with Miss Pumpkinhead. It was amazing. She told me a lot of cool stories. She said I was awesome, and that I should never change, no matter what my parents or teachers or child psychologists told me. An invisible, crushing weight was lifted off my shoulders. Before I met her, I always felt out of place, and didn't have many friends. I was never invited to sleepovers or birthday parties, and I just couldn't figure out why. Was I really *that* odd?

Miss Pumpkinhead, however, loved me just the way I was. I never felt weird or awkward around her—I just felt right and amazing and special. I made a bunch of drawings of myself and Miss Pumpkinhead. I even sculpted her out of Play-Doh. She loved it.

***

Our friendship didn't last long, though, as one day my parents got called into school. Apparently, I drew something graphic and disturbing, and the teacher got spooked. I can't remember what it was, but my parents took Miss Pumpkinhead away after that. I've never experienced such agony as I did that day. I fought to keep Miss Pumpkinhead, but my parents were merciless. 'You're a girl, not a goddamn *pumpkin!*' shrieked my mom as I kicked and screamed, but ultimately, it was pointless. Miss Pumpkinhead was gone for good.

My despair soon turned into numbness. I spent hours shaping Play-Doh into little pumpkins and hid them under my bed. I didn't talk to anyone unless I was made to. I was an outsider yet again, a nobody and a weirdo. I often cried. Not even my *Goosebumps* books or my secretly stashed horror VHS tapes could've cheered me up. I longed for Miss Pumpkinhead's company; for her gentle, soothing words. My palm felt empty without her curved shape nestled into it.

I fucking hated it.

***

Despite my parents' displeasure, I became an artist. I studied sculpture and was praised for my work—luckily, it caught the eye of a high-end gallery, which offered to represent me. They *loved* my style, they wrote in an email. Very *bold*, very *'out there.'* Whatever that meant. The only thing that mattered to me was the clay. I shaped it into smooth, round surfaces, and carved a familiar face into it. It was an itch I had to scratch to feel alive.

***

Lately, I started working with organic materials. Feathers, bones, fur, dirt, all the good stuff, rolled into one big round mass. *'Very experimental,'* my gallerist told me. I was often asked what my inspiration was, but I never told anyone the truth, because it was as boring as it was painful—it was just muscle memory. Simple as that. I chased something that was denied to me long ago; something that I thought I could never have again.

Despite the lack of a sensical explanation, people ate it up. *Dark and edgy*—one art critic wrote. *Makes you feel unpleasant, like something's going to jump right out.* I was starting to get pretty popular. But even though almost every sculpture was sold, I wasn't satisfied. Meat and vegetable peels and honeycombs didn't cut it anymore.

The medium just wasn't right, and my fingers have started to become jittery.

***

One night as I was getting ready for bed, my eyes began to itch.

What started off as a small tingling soon became a sandpaper-like agony: they itched and itched no matter how much I rubbed and probed at them, eyelids burning up underneath my fingers. My head throbbed like it had its own brutal pulse. I looked in the mirror and screamed— red, blotchy shapes spread across my face. I panicked. My nose and eyebrows and cheeks burned up, prickling with a taut pressure. Something was shifting underneath my skin, stretching and convulsing. My face felt strange: like a foul, gross cling film I had to rip off immediately. It was suffocating me, and I suddenly knew what I had to do. I retrieved a knife from the kitchen and began to work.

It wasn't easy, as the blood kept falling into my scratched eyes, but I kept going. After all, it really *was* all muscle memory. Skin and teeth and cartilage filled the sink. Metal blade scraped against bone. I kept carving and carving away, impatient to see the end result.

As I sliced, I finally remembered what that drawing I made as a kid was, the one that the stupid teacher freaked out over. I laughed even though it hurt to do so. A shape started to emerge—blood orange and smooth as I took a razor out to even out the surface. Dark, triangle pits of eyes shined as I grinned into my reflection, toothless once again. All the doubt and anxiety was long forgotten. I only ever needed to carve her out. Miss Pumpkinhead stared right back at me, giddy and teary-eyed, and I finally knew what the right medium was.

Knife in hand, I headed to the door. There were many more Miss Pumpkinhead's out there to set free.

Creepy Stuff Happens in Nowhere: An Ode to Courage the Cowardly Dog

Essay by Xochilt Avila

Have you ever looked into the unknown?

When I was five years old, my mom shucked me into a car and drove us from our LA home to somewhere in the middle of the desert. Apparently, we were in the outskirts of Menifee, but to my tiny child brain it simply felt like *nowhere*. I don't know how long I was there, or even *why* I was there (though, low-key, I think my parents were fighting). My childhood memories are like flipping through an old photo album. Some are stronger than others, but most are at least a little withered from time. Some come as familiar smells, or as a heaviness that suddenly clutches my heart.

But there's one memory from that time that shines crystal clear. It was the midnight hour. I was standing outside of some relative's house, gazing into the night sky and the endless darkness. Starlight bounced off my eyes. Residual heat tickled my skin while a gentle breeze carried over the stench of the chicken coop. It was beautiful. It was terrifying. And it seemed to go on *forever.*

My younger self couldn't understand how not even a million balls of burning gas could beat back the inky darkness that swallowed everything. There were no street lamps, no nearby neighbors to shine light out from their porches or windows. It was just us. It was like the rest of the world had disappeared. All that remained were the shadows, and all the secrets that lurked within them; monsters, murderers, dangers my mortal mind couldn't even begin to comprehend.

It was, perhaps, my first *real* experience with the unknown. And, terrifying as it was, it entranced me to chase and seek out more of it.

Fortunately for little ol' me, my next dance with the unknown would come soon after. And I wouldn't even need to be dragged out of my home. I'd live it vicariously through a tiny pink dog on my television screen.

Of course, I'm talking about *Courage the Cowardly Dog*; a show that stands as a pillar of my childhood and one of my earliest experiences with horror.

For those unfamiliar, *Courage the Cowardly Dog* is a '90s animated comedy-horror created by John Dilworth. Stemming from a seven-minute short, the series snowballed into four successful seasons and a couple of movies. It centers on Courage, a sweet but terrified dog, who lives with his owners: the sweet Muriel and horrendous Eustace. The trio live on an isolated farm in Nowhere, Kansas; their house is only accompanied by a creaking windmill, an endless horizon of sand, and a vicious onslaught of incredible, diabolical villains.

As an anxious child, I often slept on the couch next to my mom, too afraid to sleep alone in my room. Thus, I often stayed up far too late in front of the television. This was how I met Courage, and I still remember squirming as I anticipated what monster would torture him that episode. As someone so often scared, so in fear of what I couldn't anticipate, I felt deeply for the poor little pup and the horrors he faced.

Like many shows of that era, Courage leans on the classic "Monster of the Week" schtick. But where it shines is just how *unique* its villains are. From such antagonists as pig-chefs serving human hamburgers, to a (bad) CGI ghost of a dead Egyptian pharaoh, Courage is a smorgasbord of weirdness. And it's that weirdness that makes the show so damn special.

From *Goosebumps* to *Are You Afraid of the Dark?*, the '90s was absolutely ripe with terrifying kids' shows. I *adored* these shows. But Courage was unsettling in a way that I'd never experienced before. The episode "Heads of Beef" introduces Jean Bon, an anthropomorphic pig who owns a diner and (supposedly) grinds humans up into hamburgers. It's a fantastic concept, so exaggerative and playful. But it's also eerie. The tiny diner is like a pocket dimension, the blank windows indicative of the isolation of Courage's home. Jean Bon torments the poor pup at every opportunity, flashing crooked smiles in his blood-stained apron. "I'll hold it 'til he gets back," Jean muses as he carries away a customer's suitcase, only to return with the man's face imprinted on a burger. Jean and his diner are as hilarious as they are uncomfortable, as familiar as they are foreign.

All of the episodes are like this; a balancing act between camp and uncanny. Though some episodes tilt closer toward the dark, you never know which way the pendulum might swing. "King Ramses' Curse" features a ghostly pharaoh obscured in fog who plagues Courage and his family until Eustace returns his ancient tablet. This is one of the few episodes that incorporates CGI, which cleverly adds to the discomfort that Ramses' ghost invokes. As a child he *terrified* me, and for years I couldn't escape the memory of his cries to *return the slab*. Embarrassingly, I sometimes imagine it now, and it quickens my steps as I head upstairs for the night.

Courage the Cowardly Dog is such a unique experience, and while it has likely inspired many shows and projects, I doubt we'll ever see such ostentatious experimentation with villains, animation styles, and the human fear of the unknown. If you've never seen it, I implore you to seek it out. I'm not sure if I'll ever fear the unknown like I did watching Courage on my parent's couch, or gazing into the pitch-black darkness of the SoCal desert.

But on that note, I *am* visiting my folks in a couple of weeks, who've retired to the mountains of central California. Perhaps I'll glimpse into the unknown again. Perhaps I'll step out onto the deck that overlooks the chicken coop, and I'll breathe in the nostalgic smell of farm and dust and clear, crisp air. Perhaps I'll stare into the darkness and anticipate for myself anything and everything that might emerge. Because creepy stuff happens in nowhere.

Memory Is a Viewfinder

by Jenny Lewis

"*Chk*. Christmas 1994," I say to Jocelyn, my therapist, as I hold the imaginary toy to my face. I can almost feel the plastic against my nose. The cool rings around my eyes. "First pair of roller skates: Ice Princess white with shiny magenta wheels." Asphalt burn and shells stuck in the skin of my knees. I push my finger down.

"*Chk*. Summer 1995. Family vacation to the Grand Canyon. A beat-up camper. Forced proximity and happiness, the trip was a Band-Aid for a broken back. I fell asleep under the stars listening to my mom's desperation; her sobs filled with a hopelessness that I would only come to understand much later.

Chk. October 1996. I'm at the edge of Juniper Pond; my new hightop LA Gears—neon-pink-and-green gills—sink into wetland mud. Fist curled. Knuckles white, body vibrating—electric and untethered. Thunder rumbles in the distance. The sun is gone, hidden behind the looming Nothing. Heat lightning illuminates the darkness like a strobe light on Halloween. The wind blows wild through the weeping willows lining the pond.

Tears welling in my eyes, I open my mouth to scream but the world is silent—my fevered yowl somehow deafening even to myself. Breath heaving. Body shaking. The cool rain drenches my skin. And there, in the middle of that wretched watering hole, amongst pink flowering buds, a head rises from beneath the suffocating duckweed. Scraggly layers of algae-covered hair. Sunken into her skull, two glowing yellow eyes stare back. I take two careful steps away, but slip and fall, wet earth splashing the backs of my legs, my palms caked and slippery. Water gurgles—tar-pit thick from beneath the thing in the water. Her eyes shift in astigmatic fervor. The glowing intensifies as the half-head floats closer. My legs bicycle backwards, slipping, sliding against the wet soil, but I get to my feet.

She stops. I watch her watching me. My pulse steadies. My fear dissipates, a wistful sadness in its stead, and she slips back beneath the water. Lightning cracks; its threat sends me running. Crying. Confused. And eager to see her again.

Chk. Home is almost as dark as the storm. Quiet, a silent sadness permeating its core. Dad is working again—a nine-, ten-, twelve-hour shift—more ghost than parent. Kerrigan, my sister, has made meatloaf again.

I say, *Mark Hawkins stole my bike. I had to walk. I went to Juniper Pond and …*

She's angry. Scared too. *There are signs, Jessie! It's dangerous.* But she plays it off, sticking green beans under her gums and between her fingers. She cackles. *Jenny Greenteeth will snatch you up!*

We laugh like Sunday afternoon in the pool.

Chk. I cut class after lunch the next day. I pick wildflowers: Thistle (it pricks my finger) and Queen Anne's lace. Cypress and fern. At the edge, I wait—my heart plunges at her absence. Walkman on my jeans, I press play, dig a hole, and place the homemade potpourri in it as an offering as I sing "Wonderwall."

The song ends and she's there—not two feet from me. Water to her shoulders, an ancient, emerald goddess. I want to jump into her arms—hug her. To see if she's real (of course she is.) She closes her glowing eyes and inhales my gift. A cacophonous 'thank you' leaves her rotten lips.

I tell her about Mark and the kids I can't relate to. About the girls who laugh at my sadness. About Dad. About Kerrigan and the meatloaf and her horrible impression, but she smiles—rows of razored yellowed fangs—and we laugh so hard I fall back into the weeds, staring at the cotton-candy clouds, straining to breathe.

Chk. Every day at the pond: I bring Jenny Pop-Tarts and Bugles and put them on my fingers so we can be twins. I show her a drawing of Dad and Kerrigan in the house, and me and Jenny holding hands outside it.

We can be friends forever, I say.

We skip stones. Water rippling. I tell her about Brandon, a shy boy in my class. I show her how I pretend to kiss him on my hand and all the games of MASH in my notebook. She's more of a listener, her vocabulary a series of clicks, guttural growls, off-key singsong, and the occasional wail. But I understand her. Green pustules seep out of her glowing sockets when she looks at me. Like we'll never share a moment like this again. Deep down, I feel it, too, but the sun is shining, the blue sky stretching for miles, not a cloud in sight. *Chck. Chck. Chck.*"

My smile fades.

"Did you run out of memories?"

"No. Sometimes the slides get stuck. Blank—just a sliver of an image in the corner." I place the imaginary viewfinder in my lap.

"What really happened that day, Jessie?"

"October 28, 1996. It was humid. Hot for late October. Mark stole my bike and I ran off, angry. I ran until I came to Juniper Pond. A woman in a floral dress floated at its center. At eleven, I knew what drowning looked like. (In Florida you learn to swim almost as early as you learn to walk.) But it wasn't that. Not really. Vultures circled above." I pause, taking a deep breath. "I dove into the brackish muck. Thrashing, I grabbed at her. She bobbed, teetering until she was right side up. Her body rigid, her face like one solid bruise. Veiny. Eyes, cataract white." I shiver.

"'Mama!' I cried. 'Mama!' I heaved us backwards kicking against the vegetation strangling my feet, her lifeless body heavy on top of my small frame. Somehow, I got us out. We laid there, on the bank of Juniper Pond, until the sun was almost gone. Until the sirens came. Until my father wrapped his warm arms around me.

"Sometimes the truth is hard to see."

I pick up the viewfinder. "That's why I remember Jenny."

GROWING UP HORROR

ESSAY BY CANDACE NOLA

I was always the spooky girl, which I suppose makes me a bit odd knowing how often I had nightmares as a young child, but by the time I was seven or eight years old, I was a firm fan of ghost stories and other horrors. My father often told us ghost stories from his younger years, both real and imagined, as he was raised in a very active haunted log cabin as a child. He had some real scary stories to tell, all of which were corroborated by extended family. We heard a lot of scary stories around campfires too, as that was a favorite family vacation for us. We spent most of the summers camping all along the east coast.

We were raised on the idea that ghosts were real, that spirits lingered here with us, not ready to move on or not able to understand that their time had come. Ghosts were as real to me as our dog was, as accepted as the existence of air was; we could not see it, but we breathed it all the same. My parents were paranormal investigators during my young adult years, but they had always been into that lifestyle and belief, especially my father, considering the activity in the home he was raised in.

For the curious among you, being a member of a ghost hunting family wasn't always as exciting or as bizarre as some people might think. Our house wasn't haunted (much), at least not until I was an adult. We didn't go to bizarre locations every night of the week or hold seances. We were a normal family, 98% of the time. My father worked in one of the last steel mills in the region. My mom was a normal housewife, having retired from work by the time they decided to really form a ghost hunting team. I was older, working, and had kids of my own.

When my father began talking about doing paranormal investigations, we were naturally all in. He began buying the equipment, studying what each one was used for, reading up on protection prayers, demonology, occult studies and other such texts to prepare for whatever entity we might cross, and he started looking for other like-minded people to form a team with, outside of our family. Before too long, Springhill Paranormal was formed.

We normally held investigations on weekends to better accommodate the late-night hours for the overnight hunts that we went on. My father planned the trips to each location; sometimes old graveyards that he had gotten access to, or a private home with a lot of activity as noted by the owners, private estates that were hot spots and old state asylums were the most common spots. Once the location was chosen and a time set, we let the other team members know and would meet them there.

Our investigations followed a specific procedure for our safety and the safety of anyone that may be with us, typically beginning with an equipment check prior to leaving for the location. Flashlights, extra batteries, the laser grid, a couple laser pointers, several automated voice recorders, the EMF detector, and the EMF detector speaking box. This was another type of EMF device that had a red light and a green light on the top. This allowed communication with a spirit by asking a yes or no question that the spirit could answer by lighting up the red or green light. This was done simply by the spirit hovering near the red or green light or touching it.

Once the equipment was checked, we checked ourselves. Soft clothing in dark colors, preferably black, cell phones set to "do not disturb," our own flashlight and 1-2 glow sticks, voice recorders of our own, water bottles and snacks. Snacks and water were necessary as most of these hunts took several hours and were usually old, empty places with no running water. Once at the location, equipment would be divided between the team members and then my father would say a protection prayer for all of us, prior to stepping onto the location grounds, so whatever we might encounter could not attach itself to us.

Before going inside any location, we discussed the rules. Respect the property. Respect the spirit world. Respect the hunt. Respecting the property is simple enough to understand, no matter the condition of the location, we would not be causing further harm, destruction by littering, breaking things, or doing anything to cause lasting damage. Respect of the spirit world has several meanings: do not provoke any spirit, under any circumstance, and do not attempt to mock, anger, or intimidate any spirit that may be inhabiting the location.

And the last rule, respect the hunt. Ask respectful questions of the spirits. Do not make excessive noise when other team members may be investigating near you. Do not leave your assigned area until the noted time, unless it's an emergency. This was to help keep the noise level down and make it possible for other hunters to have a more successful experience.

Once inside, we would meet with the owner, caretaker, or a guide, and get the history of the location, the layout, and the noted hotspot. Then we would be left alone to set up our investigation. We would normally walk the building as a group, set up voice recorders in different spots, and decide where each team would go, as we typically split up into teams of two to investigate different areas.

After we settled into our assigned area, the actual investigation would start. We would walk the hallways and various rooms, spending time in each spot while asking questions with the voice recorders on, waiting for any sounds, any type of shadow, any response at all. We would look for shadow figures, listen for any possible noise in response to our actions, take steps to record it as activity and then try to debunk it. We checked for water pipes, radiators that were still operating, signs of rodents in the walls, tree limbs scratching on outer windows or doors. Ghostly activity can often be attributed to these normal occurrences. Once we had ruled everything else out, we recorded it as a possible paranormal occurrence.

After so long in one spot, we would move on and meet in the break room or lobby area, fill the others in on what we heard, felt, or experienced, and then switch areas. New locations, new sets of eyes and new personalities; sometimes, certain people on the team were more sensitive to the sounds or shadows. Other times, it seemed that a spirit just liked a certain person more and would be compelled to answer their questions or interact with us. My father often received responses, and my daughter was well-liked by many spirits. She would get a lot of activity around her or responses to the EMF question box.

When the hunt concluded for the night, we would gather for another protection prayer outside the building with the intent of this prayer being to block any entity from leaving with us. We never left a location without this prayer. My father was meticulous about this step, and it went for everyone, religious or not. Some nights we noted a lot of activity; other nights, we left empty-handed.

It may sound odd, but I was never truly scared by the idea of ghosts being real. It was just accepted that they were, and most were as harmless as most people and, just like people, there were always a few bad apples. The spirit realm, the idea of demons and angels, monsters and cryptids and aliens and other dimensions, all those concepts were real to me, or at least considered to be very real possibilities in my mind. My parents kept us very open-minded to the *other* things in life, to those concepts that not everyone believed in, but for us, it was just a natural extension of life.

As I started to write horror, I realized that I had chosen it because there was so much more that I could add to the story, while keeping the core relatable for most readers. I believe that a well-written horror story can capture the essence of humanity more completely than most other types of stories. There is love within the basis of almost every horror story, whether it's romantic, familial, or friendship. The love is what guides the actions of the hero or heroine in the story.

It's normally that need to protect, avenge, rescue, or return to a loved one that drives the final survivor to fight back, to dig deep down into their primal instincts to survive whatever is attacking them. A horror story is capable of showcasing the entirety of the human spirit, by which I mean it can show fear, courage, endurance, strength, grief, love, and loss, all within the pages of a single story. But it also shows the darkest side of that nature as well, the rage, anger, hatred, depravation, and vileness that a human can hold, and inflict on another.

For me, horror will always be what I write, because I want to show readers that no matter how dark it gets, how awful things seem to be, there is always a way to survive and overcome the darkness that haunts you.

THE TRUNK

BY CANDACE NOLA

"Dad said not to touch that," Mason whispered to his brother Danny.

Danny inched closer to the decrepit old trunk in the corner of the basement.

"It's just an old trunk," Danny sneered. His tone indicated he was the older and wiser of the two, and whatever Dad said was not something he needed to adhere to.

"Danny! He said it would get out. Don't!" Mason's voice rose in pitch as he backed away. He was ready to bolt up the stairs the second Danny did whatever it was he was going to do.

"Don't be such a pussy, Mason-Dixon. Jesus, it's just an empty old trunk. See?" Danny reached out suddenly and slapped a sweaty palm on the side of it, rattling the rusty latches.

Mason shrieked at the noise and raced up the steps, not even bothering to look back. Danny's laugh followed him, loud peals and snorts that sounded like a dying donkey. In another minute, his footsteps thudded up the stairs. Mason stood at the top, watching him, eyes wide.

"Did it get out?"

He breathed as Danny reached the top, pushed Mason out of the way, and slammed the door behind him.

"Course not, stupid. Ain't nothing in there, I told you. Dad just likes scaring you."

Mason trailed Danny to the kitchen, his heart still racing in his slight frame. He could hear the pounding in his ears, like he ran too fast. He took a breath, trembling a little, hoping Danny didn't notice. But he did.

Danny grinned at him, then his expression softened a bit. He noticed the fear on Mason's face.

"Oh geez, I was just having some fun," Danny said. "Want a popsicle?"

Mason nodded, and Danny opened the freezer door and snagged two juice pops from the plastic tray. Orange for him, blue for Mason.

"Come on, let's go outside."

Mason took his popsicle, bit the plastic top open with his teeth, and followed Danny outside into the summer air. His fear was almost forgotten. Almost.

***

After a long day of riding bikes down the dirt trails by their house, playing catch in the backyard and hunting crayfish in the muddy stream past their garden, the boys laid in bed, ready to sleep and do it all again tomorrow.

There in the dark, Mason's thoughts drifted back to that morning in the basement and the mystery of the massive trunk that sat there like a sarcophagus housing an ancient mummy. What was in there exactly, and why didn't their dad want them near it? Him and Danny were allowed to do almost anything, as long as they weren't hurting each other or damaging the house.

Their dad worked long hours, and the boys often spent summer days on their own, exploring the countryside with their friends, watching cartoons, and generally doing what boys do. Except Danny liked to do things he shouldn't, and, sometimes, Danny liked to scare him.

Danny also liked to see how far he could push their father before he snapped. It wasn't just their dad; Danny behaved the same way with their teachers at school.

When they were younger, their dad told them stories about the trunk, scary stories that made Mason's arms break out in gooseflesh. Stories that made Mason have more than a couple nightmares and stories that Danny often repeated at school, but as bigger and better versions, usually with a few cuss words thrown in.

One time, their dad said the trunk held the bones of a pirate from long ago that he discovered when he was sailing with the navy. He said the trunk might hold treasure maps and gold coins, but they were never to open it because the trunk was cursed. Another time, the trunk held secret books of their grandfather: a famous warlock known for keeping witches away. That story claimed the trunk held all the secret knowledge of their grandfather, ready to be passed on to them when they were ready. Mason liked that story, more exciting and mysterious than scary.

Another time, during a violent thunderstorm, Dad drunkenly told them the trunk held the body of their mother; too beloved for him to part with, too precious to be buried underground where her tombstone stood in the churchyard. Through bottles of beer and red-rimmed eyes, he told them how she could never leave them because he kept her there, locked in the trunk. As the thunder rolled around them and lightning struck a fissure in the black sky, Mason swore he heard the anguished wails of a woman and the raspy scratch of long nails on weathered wood.

There had been many stories, some of which were repeated several times over. Sometimes, Dad made them funny. Other times, he made them extra scary. But lying in his bed now, Mason realized that their dad had never told the story about their mom again. He thought this over, trying to remember if he was right or not. He recalled how sad their dad had been that night. How his voice broke on some of the words and how he kept blinking away the wet sheen in his eyes. Mason figured that story just made him too sad. He understood that; he missed his mom a lot, probably even more than Danny did.

He sighed and rolled over, closing his eyes to sleep. He missed the funny stories his dad used to tell. He missed Danny being funny and nice. He used to be a lot more fun, but since their mom had gone, Danny had turned into the bully he was now.

As he started to drift off, a low moan rose from somewhere beneath the house and was lost to the wind outside. Mason slept fitfully that night. Maggot-riddled pirates chased him across island beaches, and long fingernails rasped across the bedroom walls like rats skittering across the attic floor.

***

In the morning, Mason got up late and went in search of breakfast and his brother. The house was silent, which meant their dad had probably gone to work already. He wandered into the kitchen and grabbed a toaster pastry from the box on the counter. Their dad always bought the cheap kind, but Mason didn't mind. Danny grumbled about them, but he ate them, too, more than Mason did. Mason didn't think Danny could even tell the difference other than the box they came in being different colors.

He opened the fridge to get the milk out, poured a glass, and set off to search the house for Danny. A few minutes later, Mason was standing at the basement door, listening to the faint noises drifting up the stairway. Danny had not been in the living room or the bathroom. That left the basement.

"Danny, you down there?"

No answer, just a persistent scratching. Mason took another bite of his pastry, swallowed the suddenly too-dry food and called for Danny again.

"Danny? What'cha doin?"

"Come on down, Mason-Dixon," Danny finally called. His voice was faint, somehow muffled, and more scratching sounds met Mason's ears. He hated when Danny called him that. He had learned about the Mason-Dixon line in school last year, and it had become Mason's newest nickname.

Mason stared down into the gloomy basement, then at the food in his hands. Sighing, he threw what was left of the pastry away and set his empty milk glass on the kitchen counter. He really hated the basement, but he hated being alone in an empty house even more. He started down the wooden steps, clutching the railing the whole way.

At the bottom, he stepped off the landing onto the cold concrete and walked into the open section of the basement. There in the corner, huddled over the trunk with a screwdriver, was Danny. Mason felt sick and wanted to run back up the stairs. Instead, he stood rooted to the floor, feeling the cold seep into his bare feet.

"What are you doing?" he asked Danny.

"Well, shithead, after listening to you whimper and cry all night about this stupid trunk, I decided I'm going to open it so we can see once and for all that it's just an empty trunk, and you can quit being a pussy about it." Danny sneered, turning to eye him with one bright blue eye.

"I wasn't crying about it last night," Mason said, confused. He remembered some bad dreams about a pirate, but he didn't remember waking up. Had he?

"Dude, you were up screaming about it—about the nails scratching, about something wailing." Danny turned to face him, screwdriver clutched in one hand. "It took me twenty minutes to shut you up."

"I'm sorry, Danny. I didn't mean to," Mason stammered, not knowing what else to say. He could see Danny was in a bad mood. He really didn't want to upset him further.

"Look, let's just go watch TV or something. I'm okay, honest. I won't be scared anymore."

"Too late, pussy. I'm going to open this bitch, whether you want me to or not. Then you'll see. You're just a pussy. And when you do see that it's empty, I want you to tell me what a pussy you are, got it?" Danny sneered, waiting for Mason to nod, then bent to the trunk again.

"Go get me the crowbar from the garage and hurry it up."

Mason stayed where he was for another minute, watching Danny fumble with the rusted latch, then turned away to get the tool from their dad's workbench in the garage. His hand shook when he picked up the iron crowbar, hefty and cool in his sweaty hand.

He went back into the basement, crossing the floor to the corner and handed his brother the tool. When another low scraping sound came from the trunk, Mason felt the blood drain from his face. He backed away from Danny and the trunk, hoping Danny didn't notice. He made it all the way to the stairs before his brother shouted for him to come back.

"Where you going?" Danny said. "You need to be here when I get this open, so sit down."

Mason stayed quiet and sat on an overturned crate far away from his brother. Sweat trickled down his spine as Danny dug at the latches, using the screwdriver, then the crowbar to try to break the locks. All Mason could hear was the rasping from inside the trunk, low and steady.

"Don't you hear that?" he asked, his voice was weak and shaky.

"Hear what, fuckface?" Danny replied, still digging at the box.

"That scratching? You don't hear that?"

"Only thing I hear is you being a little bitch," Danny sneered. Then he whooped when one of the latches popped open. "Hell yeah. One down, one to go!"

Mason shifted his weight nervously as Danny hovered over the massive trunk once more. The scratching was driving him nuts. Like nails on a chalkboard inside his skull. The more his brother dug at the ancient wood, the louder it got.

Why couldn't Danny hear that? He backed away more, scooting the crate against the stairs. Danny grunted as he dug harder at the latch. Mason could see him working the edge of the crowbar just beneath the stubborn plate of the lock.

The scratching got louder in Mason's head. He rose from the crate, inching along the wall, not wanting to see. Dread filled his gut, making him queasy. He wanted Danny to stop. Something was wrong. Something was *very* wrong. A clammy sweat covered him as a loud crunching sound filled the basement. The second latch was free. Danny turned to him, triumph in his piercing blue eyes.

Danny didn't see the trunk lid open. He didn't see the shadowy arms reach from within, nor did he see the demonic grin of their mother's skeletal face as she snatched him from where he stood. A second later, the lid slammed shut, and the latches were back in place, just as they had been before. Mason could only scream. He was still screaming when his father found him four hours later, standing in a puddle of urine, screaming a horrid raspy cry, while the sound of desperate scratching grew fainter in his ears.

Today Vegetables, Tomorrow the World!

Essay by Angela Sylvaine

For me, the horror started with a bunny. I know what you're thinking, and no, this is not an essay about *Watership Down* aka the book and movie that traumatized generations of children and financed the summer homes of many a therapist.

I'm referring to Bunnicula, the vampire rabbit so nefarious he united two mortal enemies—cats and dogs—in the fight to defeat him. This seemingly harmless bunny with two tiny fangs and a pattern on his fur resembling a cape slept all day and somehow snuck from his locked cage at night. He crept through the darkened home of his oblivious adoptive family and brutally sucked the juice from innocent … vegetables, leaving them shriveled and colorless.

If a cute little rabbit could be a villain, what other horrors might lie hidden beneath harmless facades? Perhaps the most hideous monsters hide behind very convincing masks. Sadly, as a girl in the world, this is a lesson that's important to learn early.

But was Bunnicula truly a monster? Early on in the original chapbooks, we're encouraged to question this assumption. Chester the cat is thoroughly convinced of Bunnicula's monstrousness, but Harold the dog begins to have his doubts. After they enact a plan to block the rabbit from feeding, he becomes quite ill and begins to starve.

Bunnicula isn't trying to harm anyone: he's just hungry. And it's not his choice or fault that only vegetable juice will satiate his thirst. Chester's insistence that the bunny's hunger will grow and that he'll ultimately harm the family may be nothing more than paranoia. Perhaps we shouldn't be so quick to judge those who are different from us, and perhaps that thing we think is scary is just misunderstood. Harold learned this and orchestrated a vegetable remedy to help his new friend, much to my relief!

So, Bunnicula wasn't a monster after all. In fact, this sweet bunny was a bit of a role model for this young reader. I was a very quiet and proper girl who learned early on to never make trouble, to always smile and put on a happy face no matter how anxious, or sad, or scared. This is somewhat in part due to my "North Dakota Nice" upbringing, but more so the result of growing up in a home with an abusive alcoholic.

Whoa, now, wait, did this essay just get serious? I thought we were talking about vampire bunnies. We are, we are. And we're also talking about a girl who was very careful not to make anyone mad, who tried very hard to be sweet, and perfect, and harmless. Like a little bunny, perhaps? But maybe this girl didn't have to be an average rabbit. She could sneakily read scary books in the middle of the night while her family slept, books that would help her manage her anxiety and fear by controlling it, by facing unreal horrors on the page in the safety of her bedroom. She could even grow her own metaphorical fangs.

May I tell you a secret? That girl did not become less scared. I'm SO SCARED. Of silly things, like the dark, and mirrors, and creatures under the bed. And of serious things, like the future of women's rights, the state of my country and our planet, and the health and safety of the one's I love.

But I am very thankful for Bunnicula and all the horrors that came after him, because I have been training for this for decades, and I won't go down without a bite.

COMING OF RAGE: WHEN THE TERRORS COME FROM WITHIN

To quote Graham Greene's "The Destructors," through the lens of cosmic horror film *Donnie Darko*: "it was as though this plan had been with him all his life, pondered through the seasons, now in his fifteenth year crystallized with the pain of puberty." For some horror authors, fear was the backdrop to the future, the catalyst for exploring what was to come. This section tackles the way our teen years formulate our views and tastes how those experiences inform our lifelong love of horror.

Patterned by a Million Eyeholes

by Nick Mehalick

The afghan covers two young boys, knees to chests on an ancient rocking chair. The afternoon is bright, the TV room dark and cold. Autumnal color wanes outside while all has left the faces of the two doing something under cover they know they shouldn't. Hands search each other for comfort, eyes closed to the monster on screen.

From pianissimo to crescendo, blood flows and *Darkside Tales* play on, moving one to go home—live with night terrors—while the other finds more boys to watch the monster leave the closet from under blankets and leaves green, red, and gold.

Why Fear the Darkness When You Could Embrace It?

Essay by Avra Margariti

It would be easy to pinpoint a single book or film that made me realize I'm a fan of horror; a single work of fiction that was my starting point in loving darker themes and the characters who succumb to the darkness, embrace it, or overcome it. But the truth is, I come from Greece, a country that is so steeped in eerie stories as part of the fabric of everyday existence, ghostly superstition, and a mix of mythology and folklore populated by strange, monstrous creatures, that I was exposed to "horror," in the broader sense of the term, much earlier than my first novel or movie. Although I do have a fond childhood memory of convincing my very religious, very old-fashioned Greek grandmother that the copy of Stephen King's *Pet Sematary* I wanted her to buy me at the bookstore was actually an animal adventure story written for children. I finished the whole thing in a single night, then bought the next horror book I could get my hands on.

I wrote my first horror story when I was eleven, about a girl who dies and becomes a ghost but isn't aware of her ghostly nature, confused as to why people are scared of her every time they see her, and growing lonelier with each new haunting. One element of horror that has always intrigued me is the concept of monstrousness, not only as an external antagonist or dark force that needs to be defeated through the characters' resourcefulness and ingenuity, but as something that lives inside every one of us. I am drawn to characters grappling with their own monstrousness, their inner demons they must address or learn how to *un*-repress. The Gothic tradition especially is good at addressing the monstrous feminine, the beautiful and the grotesque, the profane and the profound. And, of course, Greek mythology is full of women who are beasts or spellcasters or murderesses, with strong story arcs and a narrative focus of their own—I was, perhaps, a bit gay for Circe and Hekate, growing up.

Stories where your body does not belong to you, your body is changing in new, peculiar, and mysterious ways, your body is a matter of debate, paternalism, or morbid curiosity outside of your control are also of particular interest to me. This might be because of my intersecting identities as a queer, fem-presenting, disabled person having to navigate an oppressive society. Even as a child, I loved following horror stories where the subjugated character broke the ties that bind through violence, through unleashing a monstrous form or force (which they had perhaps originally feared or tried to suppress) against their jailers. For example, a final girl taking the weapon of her would-be killer and turning it against him. Or a queer-coded character, who has been called a monster all their life, snapping and giving in to the darkness inside, to nature vs nurture, and defending themselves against the bullies.

Of course, monsters are also plenty fun on their own, even without underlying metaphor and intention. Sometimes you just want to growl menacingly and claw at things—it's therapeutic, a reminder of a time when humans communicated their wants and needs more intuitively, like animals do (because what is a small child but an animal learning to be human?) Movies like Tim Burton's works and *The Addams Family* are a good reminder for children that spooky things don't have to be something to be avoided in fiction, and that darkness can be processed in healthy, thought-provoking ways.

My goal with my story "Red Riders" was to combine several of the above themes. The "final girls/queer youth gang" trope was a perfect match for "monsters as an outside force but also as an inner demon," as it allowed me to explore complex character dynamics regarding solidarity, justice, conflict, and selfhood. We all want to be seen, seen at last, even—or especially—through a grotesque transformation; to fix the mistakes of the past and address the circular nature of trauma, until horror becomes redemption.

RED RIDERS

BY AVRA MARGARITI

I fall asleep on my embalming table and dream the Wolf is back.

When I resurface, my face centimeters from the corpse whose innards became accidental conduits for my augury, I know we're in trouble.

***

My girlfriend works at the nightclub tonight. I ignore Artemis's neon-outlined coworkers who spot me hurrying through the crowd. Normally, I'd head to the bar for a chat, but I'm in my chemical-reeking mortician's robe, and red lances my vision no matter how I blink.

Artemis twirls on the pole, skin glittering around her pentagram bralette. She goddess-prances around the stage for her captivated audience, then does a geeky little wave when she notices me. I'd be swooning if I wasn't so terrified.

Dressing room, I mouth, and vanish across the dancefloor.

Artemis sits at her dresser in a silk robe, wiping off her makeup. "Maria, I thought you'd be at the funeral home."

We're the only ones around, and I'm grateful; I don't have to mask the welling of tears. "He's back," I say, "or he will be, and soon."

"Baby, who's back?"

I wipe errant glitter from her face. My fingers trail to her temple. "It'll be easier if I show you."

I let the dream trickle back. The howling. The pain. Red as our hoods used to be. Red as blood spilled on the streets of Athens.

"Oh," Artemis says, her mouth fear-small.

The Wolf, the monster we thought we'd killed when we were younger, is back for revenge. And we're completely unprepared.

***

We were a girl gang at university: Artemis, Pavlina, and I. Called ourselves the Red Riders, getting lost and found on secondhand bikes through our city's concrete, steel woods. We shared a small apartment, full of mold and water stains, where we cooked stews, practiced spells, and *loved.*

When the trail of dead women shredded to pieces indicated a Wolf roamed our city, we donned our red hoods, picked up our weapons, and became the hunters.

Red lips, red bikes, red blood.

Oh, I remember.

***

The 24-hour supermarket clerk looks at our chalk, candles, and salt bags, and shrugs. There are stranger things than two panicking, semi-retired witches doing 3 a.m. shopping.

Artemis and I walk home in the dark hand-in-hand, and I don't know which of us is trembling hardest. Her touch has always been offered so graciously, never more than what I could handle.

"Why now?" Artemis muses. "He was supposed to be gone."

"Everything happened so fast the night …" The night Pavlina died. "Perhaps the ritual went wrong. Perhaps he wasn't really gone, just—"

"Licking his wounds."

At home, we empty our bags onto the coffee table and lock somber eyes. We're going to summon Pavlina's ghost. After all, she was the Wolf's last victim, the tragic martyr when we should've all been final girls together. If anyone can help us locate the Wolf's weak spots, it's her.

Artemis gazes nervously at the blank floor-space, sofa and table pushed aside. It's the same apartment the three of us rented back in our girl-gang days. The same room where sweet, troubled Pavlina died. We've kept her old bedroom intact as a shrine to her. At least her preserved belongings come in handy enhancing the spell.

I've already reinforced the wards over our door and windows shielding us from ill-intentioned spirits or stalkers following Artemis home from work. But spirit summoning isn't everyday magic. I'm always putting barriers between me and the dead. If I let every funeral-home spirit flood my head with memories, I'd lose my mind. Just because I once survived the Wolf's mind control doesn't mean I want a repeat performance.

My muscle memory draws a summoning circle in thickly swiped chalk and delicate sigils. Artemis kneels on the floor beside me. Almost dawn. This wasn't how I wanted our day to go. I'd have massaged Artemis's high-heels-aching feet, made spice tea, cuddled. So much for a quiet night in.

"Ready?" I light the candles and settle back.

Artemis nods. "Think of Pavlina, call her to our circle. Got it."

Her hand is clammy in mine. I close my eyes and manifest Pavlina's cigarette brand, her chest binder, her Hello Kitty keychain. Pavlina, stuck forever at twenty-one. Pavlina, the perfect roommate, always arranging movie or board game nights when we were sad to cheer us up, who put everyone else before herself, hiding her sadness under smiles, her intrusive thoughts under jokes, her dark truths under white lies.

Pavlina, who let the Wolf in.

My last memory of her is a rictus scream while she fought the Wolf's possession. While she failed.

The candles are snuffed, though there's no draft in the room. I say in the reassuring voice I employ for the families of the deceased, "Pavlina, welcome—" Back? Home? "We have questions for you."

Artemis screams. The sound chills my bones. Instead of Pavlina's familiar form, a shadow-mass of teeth, claws, and fur writhes inside the summoning circle.

Something went horribly wrong in the ritual to have summoned the very creature I was trying to escape. The beast opens yellow eyes which lock onto mine. Then it lunges.

The howls resound in my head, red-hot and branding.

***

"You're lucky the wards around the apartment were so strong," Artemis says as I come to.

I groan, the bedsheets cool against my heated body. She gently lays a wet cloth over my forehead.

"What happened?" I croak.

Buttery sunlight bathes the room, banishing shadow beasts—but for how long?

"You fainted and disturbed the chalk enough for the Wolf to escape. He broke our window," Artemis says wryly.

The beast looked so different from the one in my memory, same as the people I embalm look; like a specter of their living selves. "We're alive."

Artemis taps plum-painted nails to her lips, perplexed. "I'm sure he'll be back tonight. Remember last time? The wards can hold him off, but he has other tricks to make us come out."

Or let him in.

He'll rage and lash, and when he can't break down the walls, he'll find a way to get into our heads.

"We need a new plan. If Pavlina's ghost really is gone, we can't count on her knowledge to defend ourselves. We must attack first."

I remember Pavlina and I bonding over us being genderqueer. How we thought there was no word for it until we found it together—a revelation.

I remember how Pavlina's lips tasted red and sweet like strawberries. When I didn't want to go further, I watched her and Artemis make love on our overstuffed sofa, Artemis never letting go of my hand as her body melted against Pavlina's. They made me feel accepted, even when I only wanted a fraction of the affection they desired.

So much history. So much pain. I remember.

He watched us from street corners in the yellow streetlamp haze. He was nightmare-wrought—a manifestation of thought and intent—a monster growing stronger with each man hurting another girl. His claws and teeth weren't enamel and keratin but greed and malice. His fur, flesh, and bone were shadow, but no less real.

We were stupid, young, idealistic. We thought our nail-studded bats, butterfly knives, and hedge-witchery were enough to fight him. We followed him to his lair behind the dumpsters that smelled like rotting trash mid-summer. The Wolf gave chase as predators do when they spot their natural prey.

He came for us later that night.

Seven years later, we've known enough pain to learn to be cautious. Cunning.

Artemis lights the last of the candles. We arrange them on the dancefloor, swept clean from the night's crowd. I've never been to the club after closing, the colorful strobe lights asleep and the stools upside down like dead hands reaching ever upward.

"I don't think this is the emergency your boss meant when she gave you the spare keys."

Artemis shrugs, casual-like, but I can tell she's shaking. "Being haunted by a bloodthirsty shadow monster is emergency enough."

I wrap my cardigan around my girlfriend. She kisses me, with lips but no tongue, just as I like it.

Luring the Wolf into the club after-hours was her idea. It's neutral ground, someplace the Wolf's never visited, and that gives us an advantage. It's also away from the apartment, where Pavlina's memory lingers, making me susceptible to mistakes.

I finish drawing the newest chalk circle under magical concealment. Artemis has her own witchy weapons to expel the Wolf, ones I don't know about. Last time, the Wolf tried to use his mind control on us and turn us against one another. It's good to have some aces up our sleeves.

We have our trap and our weapons. Now all I must do is lower the wards and invite the Wolf in. It'll be my choice, unlike last time.

"Ready?" Artemis asks.

I unclench my jaw. "As ready as I'll ever be."

Artemis loves this club, and perhaps it loves her back enough to protect us both within its walls, its psychic footprint. I drop the protection, casting a spell from deep within my sternum to amplify the summoning call.

The Wolf appears without preamble: no gnashing teeth and clicking nails this time, no taunts or threats. Just shadow spreading within the hidden circle, reassembling itself into a darksome, hunched form. Jaws unhinge grotesquely around the shape of my name, a pair of eyes fixing me with pleading intensity.

And as Artemis stabs the Wolf with the herb-magic-charged knife she's produced from her hoodie's pocket, I scream loud enough to wake the dead—

"Stop!"

I remember how we stayed up all night after we disturbed the Wolf's lair seven years ago. We knew he was coming, but he made us sweat first, the three of us locked inside, pacing, muttering spells of protection we didn't have enough power to cast.

How the Wolf showed outside our ward-protected door, all might and menace. But we had no way to shut his voice out, shadow-slinking against our ears, invasive, intrusive.

Little Wednesday Addams, his voice spewed poison into my ears. *Ask yourself why you're studying to become a mortician. You and I aren't so different. Death is pretty and so are the girl-corpses on your steel bed, hmm?*

"Don't listen to him!" Artemis told me, clutching my hand.

The Wolf turned to her next. *And you. You like being adored, admired, watched in a crowd. Yet you've chosen a girlfriend who calls herself asexual and won't touch you in bed. How long until she abandons you?*

"No, I love you," I told Artemis, whose eyes were teary, but her shoulders set in determination. We held on, strong in our bond. But Pavlina … Pavlina stood afar from us, trembling under the Wolf's words.

You act so sweet, so helpful. What do you fear your friends will discover? Do they know why your father's in jail? You're the same as him; same fantasies about hurting women. Is that why you dream of being a boy?

"No!" Pavlina thrashed. We tried to reach her, but it was too late. Her convulsions knocked the candles down, disturbing the salt-and-chalk shields.

Pavlina's blood-bitten lips whispered through the Wolf's possession, "Come in."

I can't stop remembering. If you forget one dead girl, or not-quite-girl, you forsake them all. You become the next target, next one in line to be skinned and violated, the flesh consumed, the heart saved as a delicacy for later. But you also forget where you stand, your history, your missteps along the way.

Stop. Go back. Don't repeat the same mistake twice.

"Wait!" I yell. "Can't you feel her?"

Artemis is shaking, her hallowed knife falling from her fist. "Pavlina."

The girl we thought gone, possessed into attacking us with teeth and nails, then killed in self-defense while the Wolf's spirit was still inside her, thus banishing them both—*our girl is back*. I break the summoning circle, and Pavlina flees with a heart-wrenching whimper.

I look around the empty club, the door hanging open. "We've been casting the wrong spell."

Artemis, pale, drawn, *fiercely determined*, nods. "It's our fault she's become like this."

We owe it to her to return her to how she was before her death. Before the Wolf.

Artemis and I wander Athens, limned in street-and-starlight, avoiding trash and cracks in the pavement. Our weapons are back at the club. We don't need them anymore, now we know what we're dealing with. Pavlina's psychic footprint is red and sweet as a strawberry.

Pained howls resound behind a row of bushes in the city park. The dark penumbra of our Pavlina's new form is bleeding in gray tendrils from the wound Artemis's knife inflicted.

"Sorry for stabbing you," Artemis says sheepishly. "*Again*. But I had to protect Maria, like last time."

We'd thought Artemis landed the blow that killed Pavlina back then, but now we know it only vanquished the vicious spirit inside, merging Pavlina with this ghostly wolf-body.

Pavlina bellows, raising her lupine head to look at us with eyes that are yellow and strange yet still familiar. Pleading. Apologizing for things long past.

"It's okay," I say. My fingers stroke her cool, misty form. "You can rest now. Will you let me help?"

Her howl says yes, but her eyes are still staring at us, beseeching. *The Wolf recognized darkness in me, I'm sorry,* she says, half-Pavlina, half-growl.

"It's alright," Artemis answers, our fingers overlapping across coarse fur. "This wasn't your fault. Not now, not then."

Pavlina sags, as if hearing the words she needed. The guilt that kept her haunting this earth, unable to move on, has been soothed. Pavlina nuzzles our palms, then disappears into ether. A sob escapes me. Is this closure? And if so, why does it feel so much like agony?

"Let's go home," Artemis murmurs. "We should honor her memory. Have her favorite ice cream, watch her favorite rom com. She's at peace now."

We walk through our city with slow footsteps, our elongated shadows entwined like two dandelions growing between pavement cracks.

There will be more wolves, hungry and howling. There will be Red Riders: girls running wild, and girls running scared. There will be friends, lovers, and roommates; guilt for inviting the Wolf in. There will be sacrifice to keep the Wolf at bay, spells of protection we know by heart, and new witchcraft we'll invent to protect the ones we love.

I Grew Up Haunted

Essay by Die Booth

I grew up haunted.

I think, really, I was haunted way before the ghosts came. I suspect that was just the way for quiet kids born in the 1970s, before neurodivergent diagnoses were a thing, and when "queer" was just a post-watershed punchline. There was always something not quite right, something indefinable missing from my life, and that absence, that intangible wrongness, preoccupied me more than any specter could.

I came from a very normal, very nice, working class English family, with no latent predisposition to spookiness. In fact, whilst growing up in the late '70s and early '80s in Britain did result in quite a bit of disturbing entertainment content from a young age (just look at children's TV from that time period!) my very early exposure to the purposefully macabre was limited. I think the first ghostly encounter that really impressed me was musical. Death Discs—specifically "Johnny Remember Me" by John Leyton, the BBC-banned '60s hit which my dad would play in the car along with the rest of his country music—absolutely captivated me. There was something magnetic about the eerie falsetto of that ghostly voice, singing like the sighing of the wind in the trees. More than atmosphere, there was a story there; a story of loneliness that even as a tiny child really *got* me.

Now, music influences my writing more than any other media— although it's predominantly goth music these days, the soundtrack of a culture where I finally found an escape from the soul-loneliness that was my constant companion growing up. There's so much synchronicity in this. My love of goth blossomed from my first true childhood musical love, Marc Almond, who covered "Johnny Remember Me" with Bronski

Beat in 1985. Writing this, I've just watched the *Top of the Pops* performance of it for the first time in nearly forty years, and it's so obviously gay, as was pretty much everything I was subconsciously attracted to as a young child. Now, researching the song, I discovered that the dude who co-conceived and produced it was a gay occultist who ended up dying in a murder-suicide. I couldn't make this stuff up.

Up until I was about fifteen, music and ghosts were my friends and my escape. Once I got a taste for horror, I sought it out wherever I could, seeing myself reflected back from every ghostly page and TV screen. Ghosts were outsiders, unfairly maligned and banished to the isolated fringes of society, and I identified with them. When I was nine, the TV adaptation of *The Children of Green Knowe* by Lucy M. Boston became my new obsession. I bought and devoured the book, which was even better. In this story, the fact that ghosts are friends is an explicit message, and far from being afraid of them, I wanted to be with them, in a place out of time where everything was magical and special, and boys were allowed to have long curly hair.

Another favorite read when I was a kid was *The Three Investigators* series. There was a pile of these Hardy-Boys-Nancy-Drew-esque books in the sideboard in my childhood home and I still have no idea where they came from. But, entranced by the covers, I read all of them. They were at least meant for kids—although probably kids a little older than I was at the time. They were also, in the tradition of *Scooby Doo*, adventures where the paranormal elements were always eventually explained by good ol' mystery solving. I didn't care that the ghosts weren't real. I also didn't care about Pete or the other one (or Alfred Hitchcock, whose involvement I had completely forgotten until I researched for this piece, so much for celebrity endorsement!) Those books were all about Jupiter Jones for me. The nerdy fat kid in the Hawaiian shirt—I wanted to be his best friend, I wanted to *be* him. Looking back, it was probably a crush. In my imagination, I lived there, in California. America was an exotic idea to me. Far away, mythical and impossibly glamorous, full of sunshine and excitement. I replicated Jupiter's life in my head, projected it onto my own. The field where I played became Uncle Titus's junkyard. I had a secret lair inside my mind where my bullies couldn't find me.

Even though I was assured by these stories that the ghosts weren't real, it made little difference. My favorite *Three Investigators* book was *The Mystery of the Green Ghost* which had a cover so terrifying to my baby imagination that I had to turn it face-down on my nightstand before I could sleep. In the dark, that skeletal green apparition with its clutching claws seemed to glow. Even in the daylight, it would plague my memory. Forty years later, I can still picture it clearly—the ghost enduring, whilst the details of how it was eventually, inevitably, debunked by my pretend best mate/boyfriend Jupiter's quick investigative wits, have long since faded from my memory.

Now, as an adult and an author, I find community and friendship in the goth scene and the world of indie horror. Ghosts were my best friends growing up, and I was glad to be haunted. They were different, like I was different, and even though they were sometimes scary, they made me feel less alone. Now, I hope that the queer, quiet ghosts I write about provide that same recognition, escape, and companionship to other readers.

THE TIP DEN

BY DIE BOOTH

Today is perfect.

It's October, but the sun is out and it's warm enough to just wear a cardigan. The blue sky is all covered in white frilly clouds and there's just enough of a breeze.

Today is the day I'm going to build a den in the Tip.

I'm not allowed to play at the Tip. But it's the only place where I could ever build a den as good as Jupiter Jones's. I tell Mum I'm going to the park. But when I get to the end of our road, I don't turn right for the park and the swings, I turn left to the path along the river.

I'm not really allowed down the path along the river either, because it's dangerous. The wet trees there smell like pepper. There's one that drips down to the water with silver leaves shaped like knives. Ivy wriggles round the bottom of the trunks. The river is slow and brown and shivery but you can't swim in it because there's a current. I'm not sure what that is, but it will kill you dead. I think of currants, and poison. And cake. It doesn't matter that I'm not allowed though, because it's only dangerous for stupid children who'll fall in, and I'm not stupid.

I check my watch. Part way down the first bit of the path, Gwen is waiting for me. She waves, and I wave back with my chin because my hands are deep in my cardigan pockets.

Gwen is my only friend. Nobody at school will talk to me. She's a year and three quarters older than I am and she has long hair in two bunches. I wish my hair was long like hers. But nobody talks to Gwen either, so she plays with me.

"We're playing *Three Investigators,*" I say when I catch up to her. She might be the oldest, but I'm better at making up games. "Pretend that I'm Jupiter Jones. You can be Pete."

"I don't want to be Pete," Gwen says. "I want to be Gwen."

"That's not playing it properly." I'm not really bothered, as long as I get to be Jupiter, but rules are rules.

Gwen says, "I don't care. I don't want to be a boy. I'm Gwen."

I think about it, making up new rules quick. "Okay, pretend that Jupiter Jones has a new best friend called Gwen."

Gwen nods.

My feet make a crunchy noise on the gravel that's the color of biscuits as we walk along the river path. The grass to the other side is long and bright green and glittery wet, with yellow dandelions in it. Everywhere is nice today. The bushes by the river are special. They have pink flowers with pods that explode and they smell of ripe peaches. As we walk, I drag my hands lightly along the peach bushes and, even though I know it's what they do, every time I set one of the pods off—BANG!—like a jack-in-the-box, I jump in surprise and we both laugh.

At the end of the first bit of path, there's a swinging gate. This is where there are no more fields, and with houses to the other side of the path instead. The houses are big and posh. There's a tall wall with stringy green weeds and ivy and moss all over it and fancy metal spikes on top, painted black. I pretend that behind the wall is the Beast's castle from "Beauty and the Beast." There are nettles all over the bottom part, so we can't get close enough to see through the twirly metal gate, but there's a bit of stone step through there, all green with moss, too, and interesting-looking holes in the walls.

"I wish we could build a den in there," Gwen says.

"The Tip is better," I tell her.

We keep going. I've never been this far away from home without a grown-up before. It feels good. On the river side, we pass a floating wooden platform that goes out onto the water. It looks exciting, so of course there's a big green wire fence around it. A sign says Keep off. Private. Risk of Drowning. I look at the fence and work out in my head how I could climb past it and get onto the platform on the river. Then we could play fishing. We could catch a fish and take it back to the den for dinner. But that's for another day: today, we are busy. We'll have to get something else for tea.

One of the trees is dropping little pine-cone-looking things. I start filling my pockets with them.

"What are those?" Gwen asks.

"Bread," I say. "We'll have it for dinner when we've built the den." I think for a second, then I pick some of the pink peach-scented flowers too. "Ice cream, for afters."

Gwen nods. We carry on walking.

Crows call to each other up in the trees. Some caw loudly, but some make a nice bubbly sound like they're purring. There's a lady walking a little curly black dog. We pass her on the path and I want to pat the dog but I'm afraid she'll ask why we're out on our own. But she smiles at me as we walk past and I smile back, trying to look grown-up. It works, because she doesn't say anything. I hear her calling out, "Dylan! Dylan!" when we've gone past, so that must be the dog's name. I try to remember it, in case I meet that dog again.

After the houses, the river path goes next to the graveyard. I want to go in, but we don't have time today. We have to build our den. There's a huge bridge with an arch across the path here. It's the tallest thing I've ever seen. We have to go under it to get to the Tip. After the bridge the path gets muddier until there's just a big concrete bit with cracks in the floor and piles of rubbish. "Do you think there's ghosts?" I ask Gwen hopefully.

Gwen laughs. "Only us."

I laugh too. I like to pretend I'm a ghost.

This last bit of the path before the Tip is spooky. Trees lean in and drop leaves onto the dark ground. Sycamore helicopters, and big, spiky yellow and orange and brown leaves. The yellow ones are the rarest and they're so yellow they look glowy. I pick one up to use as a light in the den. The further we walk down the path to the Tip, the slimier the ground gets. Lots of white fluffy feathers are stuck to the wet ground like spat-out chewing gum, as if something has been killed by a fox. But I can't see a body. You could tell you're getting closer to the Tip, even with a blindfold on, because of the smell. When we stop at the gate, it smells of gone-off milk and wet flannel. I get some of the ice cream out of my pocket and sniff it. The petals are already withering, red creases in the pink, so I drop them on the floor like confetti.

"We have to climb in," I tell Gwen. There's more trees around the Tip, and a big wire net fence like around the tennis courts at the big school. But the gate is just a normal barred gate like on a farmer's field and it's easy to climb over. I start climbing. I feel worried in case a grown-up sees us and tells us off, but nobody does. When we're past the fence I start to feel proud of myself, and I swing my arms as we walk across the bare concrete with weeds coming out of cracks, toward the piles of stuff.

It's like library shelves but made of rubbish. Big rubbish—not like kitchen bin potato peelings and things, but old furniture and big bits of metal and wood and broken bricks. Everything is rusty or dusty or scratched.

Gwen goes in first, to check for spiders. "All clear," she says.

"All clear," I say, too, because I like that. It sounds like we're secret agents.

We walk through the piles of stuff, and plan where to build our secret agent den.

"We need to dig a tunnel." I pick up a biscuit tin lid. It's covered in brown so I can't see what type of biscuits it used to be. "I've got a spade." I jab my spade at the muddy ground and it makes a metallic kind of *spang* sound but doesn't go in. I try again. I try lots, but the spade just gets more dented than the smelly earth does, so I throw it away with a clank into a pile of metal. "I've got a better idea."

"No," says Gwen, looking where I'm looking. She's always such a chicken.

"It's okay." I go up to the open door and inspect it. It's some kind of cupboard, but made of metal with shiny grey paint that's peeling off in places like burnt melted cheese. I pat the outside like I've seen Dad do to cars, and it makes a solid-sounding boom noise. The noise pleases me. It sounds important.

"Don't go in there," Gwen says.

I shake my head. "I'm going in."

"Then I'm coming in with you."

We both go into the metal cupboard. It's just big enough to fit both of us standing up. Gwen is a bit taller than me and it stops just above her head. It's clean enough inside, but the walls aren't smooth, they've got grooves every so often like the ones inside the oven that take shelves. I feel stupid just standing there right next to Gwen, so I reach out and try to close the door.

"Don't. You might get stuck."

"I won't get stuck." I can't close it. It's wedged open. I give it a wriggle, then a hard shake, but it just makes a rolly noise like thunder. So I put my whole weight into it and swing back hard on the door, which gives way all of a sudden, making me let go in surprise. The cupboard shakes as I fall against the back wall. And the door slams shut, with a loud wobbly noise, then a sliding scraping noise from outside. When it goes still again, I push against the door. It won't move. I think something fell down against it outside when it slammed. "Oh, no," I say.

Gwen is mad. "I told you you'd get stuck!"

I fold my arms. "Who cares anyway? We wanted a den! This is a good den."

"It's too small," Gwen says. "And you can't get out."

"It's okay. If I can't get out and I die then I'll just be able to stay with you and we can play forever. I'll never have to grow up. It'll be better. Everyone knows that grown-ups are stupid."

"No. I'm going to get you out."

I sigh, loudly. It sounds even louder all cooped up in the den. "How can you get me out? You can't touch things."

Gwen frowns, then walks backwards, half out through the stuck door. I can still see her frowny face glowing softly, sticking half out of the grey metal. "I'll fetch someone."

I kick the den wall. Somehow, I feel more annoyed at her trying to help me than scared at being stuck and starving to death. My tummy gives a rumble, like it's keen to get going. "How can you fetch someone? Nobody can see you except me."

"I'll think of something," Gwen says. Her face slides the rest of the way out of the door and when the tip of her nose disappears, it's suddenly a lot darker, and smaller, and smellier. It reminds me of bins, and how my hands smell after playing on the swings in the park. I sigh again, and hear the echo of my sigh all round my head like my breath is reminding me how cramped this is. I can't even sit down. I pull the light-leaf from my pocket, but it's not working any more—not even the least glow of yellow. Leaning against the lopsided wall, I press my ear to the metal. I hear Gwen say, outside, "I'm going to save you." Her voice is getting quieter and quieter.

I hope dying isn't too boring.

THE FAMILY BUSINESS

BY AMANDA HARD

"I can't believe anybody's scared by that stuff," Davey says. We're both eight years old, and neither of us are allowed to watch the show my daddy writes—*Tales of the Dark Traveler*—but Davey likes to make fun of it so he looks tough.

Mama said Daddy never intended to be a horror writer, but that's how I've always known him—hunched over what he calls his Smith Coronary, typing and smoking, ripping out sheets of paper and stuffing them into envelopes to mail to the network. *Tales of the Dark Traveler* is one of the highest-rated programs on the network, but none of us watch the show when it airs. Mama makes sure of that, unplugging the set after *Fantasy Island* ends. She makes sure Davey is home before the streetlights come on, too, walking him across the street to his house, because I know she doesn't want to move again and neither do I. I like my room, even though Daddy boarded up the one window and ripped out the rose trellis beneath it. He put up a unicorn poster and pink curtains, just like I wanted.

My favorite house was the one in California. Mama thinks I don't remember it, but I do. I also remember the party in the house, when the show first started and everybody wanted to be Daddy's friend, and how all the grown-ups watched that first episode on a big TV that Daddy bought special for the party. It was a costume party, everyone had on masks with horns, and Mama said they hadn't meant to scare me when I came down for a glass of water and saw all the candles and funny symbols marking a circle around the living room.

"It's just for atmosphere," Mama told me, sending me back upstairs. "Just for a lark, you know?"

Mama and Daddy were so happy for a while, but one night I woke up and heard them talking downstairs. Daddy's hands were shaking in Mama's, and he was crying, saying something about not being able to banish it, and Mama asked what in God's name they were going to do. And Daddy, when he saw me at the stairs, he just said, *Run.*

And that's what we do, for ten years. Daddy sends big white stacks of scripts through the mail, and they wait and watch the news, and when I hear one of them crying, or Daddy saying *No, no, no,* at a hooded shadow just outside the front window, I know we're going to move again. Daddy gets on the telephone, tries to quit *The Dark Traveler*—actually does so a couple of times, even throwing away his Smith Coronary—but The Dark Traveler won't quit him.

I'm nineteen when Daddy's heart gives out. Mama's follows a couple of months later, leaving me an orphan with a sizable inheritance of manuscript boxes, all containing carbon copies of the forbidden show. It's still on, of course, because nothing ever truly dies in Hollywood. It's a Sunday night and, out of habit, I start to turn off the set before the infomercials set in, but my eye catches the intro for a show I've never seen, inviting me to partake of this evening's tale from The Dark Traveler, accompanied by a silhouette of a hooded figure that moves quickly off camera as the episode fades in.

It's a cheesy anthology series, loosely hinged around a mysterious demon who slaughters children as some kind of moral retribution for bad decisions their parents make. Pure shock horror—the kind of show that eventually the upstanding members of a kinder, gentler generation will judge unredeemable, and any VHS copies still available will be relegated to the landfills. Enough children go missing each year that nobody needs reminding of the made-up horrors that lurked in the dark recesses of some sick writer's imagination, right?

You couldn't put a show like that on television these days. But of course, these days, you don't need television. Forty years after my father fled Hollywood, we have the internet, which assists the tech-savvy in tracking down all of the people who had been at that party forty years before—the people who'd made the pact with the entity that haunted a man who never intended to be a horror writer, but found himself unable to stop. None of those people want to talk to me or read the scripts I've written for a reboot of the show, but these days you don't need a network to fund you, or prime-time airspace to give life to your creations.

The Lost Tales of the Dark Traveler channel has over two million subscribers on YouTube, and a subreddit full of fan theories about the copycat murders and the actual episodes—all loosely hinged around a mysterious hooded figure who slaughters evil studio executives and famously wealthy and vile actors in their Malibu homes. None of the fans even ask for a believable motive. I think they're just happy to see horrible people get what they deserve.

I never intended to be a horror writer. But once you learn how to control your creation, it feels pretty good to bring something original into the world and let it loose. It feels a little like poetry. Or at least, poetic justice.

ON THE PAGE:
LITERARY NIGHTMARES

Some of our first brushes with the macabre were found between the pages of books (some of which we weren't supposed to read). Gothic classics and contemporary horror tales alike add the perfect ingredients to this section exploring our first literary horror finds.

WELL (D)READ

BY MICHAEL BAILEY

My sister, distant and radiant and smiling,
Turned her light to shadows I dared not follow.
Yet curiosity clawed me, relentless and raw,
And the book, worn and waiting, beckoned.

The night swarmed with an electric hum,
A humid veil shrouding the extraordinary.
And beside the dimmest cloth-covered lamp,
I held the tome offering promises of terror.
Each line carved fissures in my tender mind,
Peeling away at layers of innocence.

A red balloon drifted, silent and slow,
Its tether invisible, its pull inexorable.
The clown's eyes, wide, replaced the light,
And I understood fear as a creature alive.
Not the painted faces of mock-foolishness,
But the ever-beating ache within my heart.

Days blurred into a past now irreplaceable,
As the world tilted toward the inexplicable.
And then came another, an older prophet,
Whose words wound tight, a vice of syllables.
No sprawling terror of monstrous form—
But madness coiled in the mind's depths.

The Tell-Tale drum of guilt's cold cadence,
House of Usher's walls breathing despair.
I wandered those sad corridors of decay,
The weight of words suddenly infinite.
Isolation loomed, a ghost within, haunting;
A horror born of my own mind's creation.

Their monsters are my familiars now,
Shaped of terrors and memory entwined.
For fear is a mirror we cannot shatter,
Revealing reflections we dare not see.

Paperbacks and Language Barriers: A Lesson in Horror

Essay by Pedro Iniguez

There's something about nostalgia, looking back on cozy memories and how they shaped our upbringing, that warms the soul. In this case, it's something that had a direct influence on me as a horror writer.

My journey as a writer began in 2009, when my first story was published in a small chapbook called *The Drabbler*. Since then, I've amassed somewhere over 120 publication credits including short stories, poems, several collections, a comic book, and a novel. I've been published alongside so many respected authors I grew up reading; things I'd never even dreamed possible as a Latino kid.

And while I've been fortunate in achieving these things, I've also racked up hundreds (thousands?) of rejections. I've had major publishers show interest in my manuscripts only to ghost me. I've also had writer's block and depression and crippling self-doubt. And yet, I persist. But what made me a glutton for the pain? What began my love affair with horror? What about the genre was so powerful that it's allowed me to brave the stormy seas of publishing?

Sure, I could tell you about my first tastes of the macabre as a kid when my parents fed me stories about El Cucuy in an effort to scare me into behaving.

Or when I first watched *The Twilight Zone*, *Scooby-Doo*, *Elvira*, *The Nightmare Before Christmas*, or *Are You Afraid of the Dark?*

Maybe I could go on about my elementary school days when I first read "The Tell-Tale Heart," "The Monkey's Paw," and *Goosebumps*.

I could even discuss the movies my father forbade me to watch like Bram Stoker's *Dracula*, the *Alien* franchise, or *Hellraiser*, restrictions that only led to a stronger curiosity in wanting to watch them.

I could also aptly talk about my friend and mentor, the late, great Dennis Etchison, who believed in me and set me on the path to becoming a writer myself.

But there is one horror-related memory that stands out, one that I still latch onto and has taught me the most important quality in my writing career: persistence. And that is where my mother comes in.

As early as I can remember, my mother, Maria, would come home from a long day of work, make sure the family was fed, tidy up, and end the night by curling up in bed with a good horror novel, a cigarette, and a cup of coffee on her nightstand. It was her way of relaxing from the heavy grind of the workweek and caring for two children; a full-time job in itself.

Thinking back on it, I still vividly recall wisps of smoke wafting lazily around her as the bitter smell of tobacco and the sweet, pungent scent of old books lingered in the room. I remember ratty hardcovers and dog-eared paperbacks, their enthralling covers filling my mind with wicked wonder. There was Stephen King and Dean Koontz and John Saul, and even the occasional Michael Crichton and Thomas Harris thriller.

And though she wasn't the fastest reader, every week she devoured a new book. For years this went on. But being a Mexican immigrant to the United States, English wasn't easy for my mother. She was self-conscious of her accent in conversations, and certain words eluded her. Which is why she read. She wanted to improve her communication skills, and so she took to reading exclusively in English. And if it wasn't Danielle Steel, it was almost always horror.

Most days, she would call me over and ask me how to pronounce something or to explain what certain words meant. Sometimes I knew, sometimes I didn't. But she was always curious, always driven, like an eager student. And when she couldn't figure out a word, she'd look it up or make an educated guess based on the context of the passage she was reading.

As soon as she'd finished a book, she'd let me read anything from her towering stacks, which had at times lined the walls and dressers of her bedroom. At one point, my mom had curated quite the horror fiction library. I remember being a kid and taking a few stabs at reading John Saul's *Creature* and scratching my head. Same goes for an early attempt at

King's *The Dark Tower*. I always ended up putting the books away and throwing myself back into my comic books. It wasn't until college that I began to revisit some of the novels she'd read in an effort to connect with her.

But through the years, she never gave up trying to educate herself. She learned new words, she learned how to pronounce things, and she never had trouble reading in English or carrying a conversation, accent be damned.

My mother taught me that horror can break language barriers, that great stories can mend you after a grueling day, and that books can set you on a path toward self-improvement. Every week it was a new book, a new question, a few new words she didn't understand. But that meant there would be new stories, new answers, new words to be learned. New possibilities. This is the nostalgia that brings me joy and comfort. It's what I think about when I look back on my childhood and the origin of my love for horror fiction. Her persistence is what inspired me to keep going, to keep pushing despite the odds. This, I believe, is why I don't let anything stop me. Not the rejections, not the creative blockage, not the long nights burning the midnight oil. It's why I give myself fully to horror and why I strive to never stop as a writer. And for that, I hope my mom is proud.

THE CHAIN GANG CHILLER

BY PEDRO INIGUEZ

Jarred Quintania found it in the book cart, wedged between a cookbook from the 1950s and a tattered Soviet spy novel. He hadn't seen one in thirty years, but he vividly recalled devouring these juvenile spine-tingler select-your-scare paperbacks back in elementary school. He was, like many kids, drawn to their outlandish, spooky, monster-of-the-month covers. This one was titled *The Chain Gang Chiller*, and featured some teens in shackles as a mob of creepy prison guards closed in on them.

How apt.

He plucked it loose, found a seat beside the window overseeing the prison yard, and began to read. The story began with Mike, some high school kid from a rough part of town, just like him. Eventually, Mike got in with a group of devious 12th graders who dared Mike to do something bad to prove himself worthy of their friendship.

Jarred came to his first juncture. A choice to be made. Would he go along with the dare? Or would he ignore it?

Just for kicks, Jarred chose the dare, and Mike ended up stealing his neighbor's car.

The irony tasted bitter in Jarred's mouth. He peered out the window, down at the guys in the yard shooting hoops and pumping iron. Some of them stared back.

Grand theft auto wasn't the worst offense in the world. *Just three years,* he told himself. He'd educate himself working in the prison library, find himself a job, and become a valuable member of society.

Right. *Good one, Jarred.* Prison swallowed poor, broken saps like him whole and spat them out even worse monsters.

He crossed a leg over his knee and continued to read. Mike was sentenced to a few weeks in a juvenile detention center, which he loathed, until he took to reading in the library to help pass the time.

Jarred lowered the book. He checked the copyright page. Published in 1998. It was like a childhood roadmap to his future.

The bell rang and a surly-looking guard with dark eye circles entered the library. Leisure time was over. Jarred slid the book where he'd found it and made note to revisit it some other time. Without a word, the guards marched Jarred and the others back to their cells for light's out.

"Heya, buddy," Pauley, his one-eyed cellmate said, as he slid into the bottom bunk. He'd run over some poor kid while driving drunk a couple years ago. Lost his eye that way. And his marriage. Other than that, the old man was alright.

"Hey," Jarred said. "How was your shift at the laundry room? Still hearing noises down there?"

Pauley grumbled before succumbing to a snore-filled slumber.

"G'night, Pauley."

Jarred sank into the top bunk and pondered life as he did most nights. Tonight, he wondered what would have happened if he'd read that spine-tingler book back in school. Maybe he'd have chosen a different path in life. Just before he drifted off to sleep, he sneered as he regarded the AVENUES gang tattoo etched on his forearm.

***

After tidying up at the library, Jarred found the book exactly where he'd left it. He wasn't surprised; most inmates hadn't stepped foot in the library. Not here, not in the real world.

Pulling up his chair beside the window, Jarred flipped back to where he'd left off. The story went on and Mike met a slew of misfits in the juvenile detention center. Some were cool, some were downright bullies, and many came and went through the revolving door of juvenile justice. But they learned to get along over time. Mike's best friend was a kid named Benny who'd lost an eye in a bicycle accident.

"What the hell?" Jarred looked around. Was someone pulling his leg? Had someone printed a fake book just to screw with him? Naw. The book looked worn and ragged. No faking that. He shook his head and continued.

One night the kids snuck out of their rooms to play a game of hide-and-seek. Mike and Benny paired up to hide as the rest of the kids went looking for them. Mike proposed hiding in the library. Benny suggested the basement.

Time to make a choice.

Jarred smirked and chose to go with the basement. There, Mike and Benny stumbled upon the detention guards, garbed in red robes and huddled around a shadowy figure they couldn't quite make out. The guards chanted in tongues and frolicked around the occulted entity. When the dance was over, the guards retrieved a silver platter of assorted limbs and offered it to the shadow-thing as tribute.

What a spine-tingler, indeed. Even by today's standards, it was too gruesome for a kid's book. Jarred wondered how it wound up being published. Maybe it was a proof that never hit the market. A rejected little oddity he'd happen to chance upon by dumb luck. Whatever the case, it read like a potboiler. He licked his fingers and flipped the page. The next night, the guards came for Benny and wrangled him out of his room without explanation. Mike asked what was going on, but they darted off with his friend, ignoring his pleas.

The bell rang and the surly guard waited by the door, the bags under his eyes deeper, darker. The man looked like he hadn't slept in days.

Jarred slipped the book back in the cart and was prodded back to his cell. Once the lights went out, Jarred turned over in his bunk, and Pauley's snores cranked out like an old muffler.

He thought about home and how he missed it. Now, life amounted to eating slop, sleeping on a cot, and reading old hand-me-down books in a dusty library no one cared to maintain.

Swallowed by the prison system.

As his eyes became heavy, a pair of guards unlocked the cell door. Pauley stirred, grumbling as the guards stormed in, hooked their hands under his arms, and dragged him off into the dark.

"Hey," Jarred said. "What the hell are you doing? Where are you taking him?"

The guards faded down the same darkness that spat them out.

That night, Jarred couldn't sleep.

***

After his meal, he scurried to the library, jerked the book from the cart, and took his usual seat by the window overlooking the yard. He ran his index finger along the book until he found where he'd left off.

The next day, Mike noticed the rest of the kids acting stranger than usual. When he told everyone about Benny, they seemed to lower their heads, shove their hands in their pockets, and turn away. As the days went on, Mike caught the kids staring at him before averting their eyes. Like they were in on some secret he wasn't privy to.

On a whim, Jarred rested the book flat on his lap and looked out the window. Every man in that yard had been staring upward, unmoving. An ocean of eyes locked on him.

What the hell was happening? Beads of sweat began to dot his forehead as the veins in his neck throbbed to the beat of his racing heart. He stood and sat at another table, far from the window. From all those eyes. Now he was certain nothing in the book was a coincidence. The stolen car, incarceration, his one-eyed friend getting whisked away in the dead of night, the countless eyes staring at him. That meant that the shadow-thing in the basement …

His thoughts drifted to the rumors going around the pen. He'd always laughed, brushed them off as the ravings of bored murderers. But the stories persisted. Murmurs of strange noises emanating from the laundry room downstairs.

Where Pauley worked.

Jarred opened the book and continued to read, more out of morbid curiosity than boredom. A week went by and kids kept coming and going. Mike thought it only a matter of time before the guards came for him and he'd be fed to the shadow-thing. He hatched a plan to escape the juvenile detention center and bolt home to warn his parents.

Before Jarred could turn the page, the bell rang.

"No, no, no," Jarred said. "I need to know what happens next. How he gets out." As the guard entered the library, Jarred shut the book and shoved it down his jumpsuit.

The guard, looking more ragged than ever, motioned him out of the room. Jarred padded down the long hall, feeling every inmate's eyes boring into him, like a marked target. Did they know something? Would he be nabbed in the dead of night to be sacrificed?

Jarred entered his cell, which now sat in silence. The absence of Pauley's jovial greetings, or his thundering snores, was a painful void. Pauley's indentation lingered on his cot, like the imprints of a ghost.

As soon as the guard left, Jarred plucked the book from his jumpsuit, sat on the edge of Pauley's bunk, and got to reading. Maybe there'd be an answer waiting for him; a way to escape his doom. But he had to hurry before lights out.

Mike hatched a plan to escape the detention facility. He had pilfered a guard's key. The next choice was whether to risk getting captured in order to release all the other kids, or make a break for it and alert his parents.

Jarred chose to help the other kids.

One night, when Mike was certain the guards were gone, he unlocked his door and did the same for the others in the detention center. Suddenly, the kids mobbed Mike and turned him over to the nightwatchman, who in turn dragged him to the basement and fed him to its master in the shadows.

God, no. What a grim ending. He shook his head. The kids were in on it too? This book wasn't suitable for children at all.

Jarred retraced his way back to the last junction and chose the alternative option. He'd have Mike make a break for it on his own and try to get help. That night, as Mike unlocked his door, a pair of guards were already outside waiting for him. Once again, they hauled him off, feeding him to the shadow-thing lurking beneath the basement.

No, no, no. This was all wrong. There had to be a happy ending in there somewhere. Anywhere.

Footsteps echoed down the hall. Keys rattling.

Jarred quickly scoured the book for something that could help him, for alternatives, branching paths where he could've made a better decision. But every road led to the same outcome: to the belly of the shadowed beast.

Jarred furiously flipped to the beginning of the book. Before Benny. Before the detention facility. Before Mike stole the car. The very first choice. Yes, this had to be it. The answer would lie here.

Jarred had Mike ignore the peer pressure and walk home instead of stealing the car. The entire story changed. Mike ended up graduating, landing a great job, getting married and raising a wonderful family ...

Jarred didn't understand. This was no help. What about him? How would *he* get out of this?

The footsteps drew nearer, louder. The keys jingling madly.

Jarred ran a hand across his hair, now slick with sweat.

A guard walked up to Jarred's cell, glared at him, and ambled past.

Jarred gripped the bars of the cell door and watched the guard vanish down the hallway. Why hadn't they come for him? The book implied ...

Was there even a monster down there?

Like a revelation, something dawned on him. He'd already made an important choice and it happened long before he'd picked up any book. Jarred tossed the spine-tingler on Pauley's bed and clambered to the top bunk.

Whether the shadow-thing was real or not, didn't really matter. This prison had already devoured him, and, worst of all: the day he stole that car, he'd offered himself up as tribute willingly.

He buried his face in his hands. As the lights went out, Jarred hoped the others wouldn't hear his muffled cries.

Let Me Tell You a Story

Essay by Brian McAuley

Scary Stories to Tell in the Dark.

It's the perfect book title, really. So simple and direct, advertising not only what kind of stories you're getting inside the cover, but also how and where to read them.

I can't think of a single tome that had a more profound impact on my development as a storyteller than this one. Well, these three, if we're counting the sequels *More Scary Stories to Tell in the Dark* and *Scary Stories 3: More Tales to Chill Your Bones*, which we absolutely should. Today, I own this holy trinity of sacred tomes in a collected hardcover dubbed *The Scary Stories Treasury*, but I first discovered them as paperback volumes when I was just an impressionable youth.

One of my favorite childhood rituals involved riding my bike to the local library with my best friend, Keith. I don't remember exactly when my obsession with horror began, but I do remember that I was always scouring those shelves in search of something that would send a shiver down my spine. I found it in the shape of a giant head sticking out of the cemetery earth. He had patches of blue on his skull and a splotchy red nose. Was it a clown? Did that explain his lipless, toothy grin? But then why was he smoking a pipe? And why, dear God, was his sideways glare aimed directly at me? It felt like a dare, beckoning me to crack that spine and discover what dark delights awaited within.

Flipping through the contents revealed even more haunting imagery. Black ink that crawled across the paper like spiderwebs or living blood splatter. Gnarled human forms with sinewy hands seemed to reach off the page to grab at me. Illustrator Stephen Gammell crafted some truly disturbing images that stirred controversy and even incited book bans.

But his gruesome drawings were just bringing the words to life, so who was responsible for writing such a profane text?

The name on the cover said Alvin Schwartz, but he wasn't even cited as a proper author. The stories had merely been "collected from folklore and retold by" this man, their chosen vessel. The secondhand qualification only added to the eerie feeling that the horrors contained in this book were not of the fictional realm. These stories were passed down from generation to generation because at some point, somewhere, they actually happened. This included a few tales that were already familiar to my young imagination. Like the one where the couple on lover's lane discovered a hook hanging from their car door. Or the babysitter who learned too late that the threatening phone calls were coming from (say it with me now) *inside the house!*

Wait. Didn't that last one happen to my sister's best friend's second cousin?

Such is the evergreen nature and unique pleasure of these stories. The undeniable brush with reality that pairs so well with the uncanny imagery, especially in the more interactive yarns. Because again, these twisted tales weren't meant to be read alone in the safety of your quiet mind. They were designed to be *told* in a flesh and blood group setting. Stories like "The Big Toe," wherein a boy yanks a human toe from the garden and carries it home to his mother to cook in her dinner stew.

He found a *what* and she did *what* with it?!

One hardly has time to question the creepy logic before the owner of that toe comes calling. The story takes on a life of its own as a parenthetical on the page instructs the reader to pounce on the nearest listener and scream, "YOU'VE GOT IT!" There's something special about a book that gives you written instructions on how to scare your friends. An acknowledgement between author and reader that we're all playing together, that fear itself is a safe love language.

It wasn't just the printed words and drawings that spoke to me, as Keith and I soon discovered that our library also had the book-on-tape. We'd pop that cassette into my Playschool boombox, turn off the basement lights and throw a blanket over our heads with a flashlight lit beneath our faces. The gruff voice spoke through the speakers, spinning one wicked yarn after another. Each volume also contained songs that benefited greatly from this auditory experience. Songs about worms crawling in and out of a corpse's snout. Songs that were nasty and vulgar and utterly enchanting.

Scary Stories to Tell in the Dark is classified as a children's book, and I'm not a child anymore. I'm a full-grown adult: professional author, screenwriter, and college professor. So, have I matured past the juvenile fears that these fables once inspired?

Absolutely not.

In fact, I was recently invited to give a guest lecture on Halloween for an "Introduction to Storytelling" class. I brought my *Scary Stories Treasury* and stood before a hundred students in the grand auditorium. Dimming the lights and projecting a crackling campfire video on the screen behind me, I read one of my favorites.

"The Haunted House"

But I didn't just read it. I performed it.

Every ghostly footstep up the cellar stairs.

Every creak of the rusty door hinge.

Every breathy word from the phantom's decayed lips.

I let the story flow through me, let it possess me, and the effect in the room was palpable. Listeners were hanging on every word as we indulged in the shivery delights of this collective experience.

Because it's fun to be scared, especially in the dark.

So let me tell you a story…

Where Did You Come From, Where Did You Go?

by Brian McAuley

Emily Watkins couldn't wait for June 16th, 2001. The 8th Grade Dance was a rite of passage, a turning point from middle school into high school that she finally felt ready for. Especially because this wasn't the kind of dance where you had to bring a date. If it was, she might have been wondering whether or not Jonah Milton was going to ask her out. The goth loner had just transferred here in January, and everyone was wary of the new kid. Everyone except for Emily, who loved sitting behind Jonah in Mrs. Seitz's Language Arts class and losing herself in his long black hair.

But tonight wasn't about her new crush. It was about Emily and her three best friends going to the dance together and celebrating their transition into adulthood. Seeing the Ridgedale Middle School gymnasium transformed into a tropical oasis with rows of inflatable palm trees filled her heart with joy. This couldn't be the same place where she'd taken a dodgeball to the face last week. Colorful streamers fluttered overhead while flashing lights reflected off the polished hardwood floors. A thumping beat rattled through the basketball hoop above the DJ's booth.

"Ridgedale Middle School!" he shouted into the microphone. "Are you ready to paaartyyy?!"

Students cheered while a group of chaperones patrolled the perimeter of the gym. The teachers had made it clear at Monday's final school assembly that if anyone was caught "grinding" on the dancefloor, their parents would be called to take them home immediately. But these fears were apparently unfounded as Emily watched all the boys gather on one side of the bleachers while all the girls stayed on the other.

Every now and then, a brave soul was sent out on a reconnaissance mission.

"So-and-so wants to know if you want to dance with them."

Sometimes this offer would result in a pair of awkward pre-teens meeting at center court to shake awkwardly in front of each other for three-minute intervals. More often than not, the numbers remained unmoved on either side of the gender divide. It wasn't until a certain song started playing that the energy shifted. A furious fiddle pulled everyone to the floor, beckoning them to dance along to a song they knew all too well.

A song called "Cotton-Eyed Joe."

Like the "Macarena" and the "Y.M.C.A." before it, this choreographed dance tune was guaranteed to play at every school dance in the country. Which is why Emily and her friends had decided in advance that this would be their queue to escape while the whole gym was distracted. As the dance floor flooded with stomping feet, not even the chaperones noticed the four students slipping out the back door into the night.

A floodlight clicked on, illuminating a patch of pavement in the dark as the friends gathered behind the redbrick building. Emily was the first one to say, "I really hate that song."

"You know what it's about, right?" Dylan Marshall lit the cigarette that he'd swiped from his father's weekly carton. "My dad actually knew the real Joe. They worked together at the coal mine. Poor guy was homeless, never showered. Some people thought maybe he *lived* in the mine. Joe always showed up to work before anybody else, still wearing yesterday's soot. Adding another layer, day in and day out, until it soaked in so deep, his skin went pitch black. Until all you could see were his eyes popping white in the dark. Anyway, my dad said Joe must've inhaled too much coal dust. Started talking crazy about a demon in the mine trying to possess him. One day, they heard Joe screaming, deep in that mine. A search party went in, but his body was never recovered. Some of the other miners say he still haunts the place. If you listen real closely in the coal mine at night, you can hear him calling. *Jooooooooooooe!*"

Nita Vincent rolled her eyes at her boyfriend. "Why would he be calling his own name?"

Dylan squinted like he'd never thought about it before. "Because … he was crazy."

"Because that story isn't true." Nita took the cigarette from Dylan's hand and puffed confidently. "Cotton-Eyed Joe is just another racist stereotype in a white folk song. The singer would've been 'married a long time ago' if that cotton-picking slave hadn't stolen all the white women. They used to perform it in minstrel shows with white people wearing blackface. I can't believe they actually play this offensive trash at school."

"That's not how I heard it." Robbie Harrison swigged from his flask, filled with vodka from his mother's not-so-secret under-sink bottle. "It's not always about race, Nita."

"Says the white boy," Nita snapped back.

"All I'm saying is you're focusing on the wrong lyric." Robbie passed the flask to Emily. She kept her lips pursed as she tilted the liquid against them, pretending to gulp. Emily wasn't comfortable drinking alcohol yet, but she knew she'd get there soon. Everything would be different in high school. She passed the flask to Dylan as Robbie continued his story.

"'Where did you come from, where did you go?' That's the key. See, way back in the day, there was this old piano player named Joe. He performed at the local saloon, where he drank so much moonshine that his eyes turned milky white. Poor bastard went blind as a bat, but he kept playing, a regular Stevie Wonder. Until one night, after his set, he stepped out onto Main Street and *WHAM!* Trampled by a horse-drawn buggy. Killed instantly. But people still see Joe's ghost wandering around town. Singing ..." Robbie closed his eyes and stretched his arms out, singing along to the lyrics that echoed from inside the gym. "'Where did you come from, where did you go?'"

Nita slapped Robbie's arms down. "Don't be dumb. You can't actually drink yourself blind."

"Tell that to Cotton-Eyed Joe," Robbie responded.

"I'll tell that to Vicky Parsons, see what she thinks of your corny bedtime story."

"Whatever." Robbie blushed at the mention of his crush and snatched the cigarette from Nita's hand. "See if I care."

Emily shook her head. "I'm betting you're all wrong."

"They are." A voice responded from the shadows.

All four middle schoolers turned to face Jonah Milton. Emily hadn't spotted the boy in the Korn T-shirt earlier in the gym, but her heart skipped a beat now as he opened his mouth to say: "Cotton-Eyed Joe is something much worse."

"Okay then, new kid." Dylan moved aside, inviting Jonah into their circle. "Enlighten us."

Jonah stepped into the patch of light and bowed his head, letting that long black hair hang over his face. "The real Cotton-Eyed Joe was a serial killer. A drifter who went from town to town wearing a black trench coat and dark sunglasses. He wore them to hide his eyes … because they were both covered in white cataracts."

"Ooo, very scary." Robbie laughed. "The man with cars for eyes!"

Nita elbowed him. "Cataracts, not Cadillacs, dummy."

"Right." Robbie took a stubborn drag. "I was just joking."

He passed the cigarette to Emily, who held the burning stick between her fingers. She had no intention of smoking it, totally focused on Jonah and his story now.

"Every time Joe showed up in a new town, the local population would plummet. Because Cotton-Eyed Joe was picking them off, one by one. Until one day, Joe landed himself in the wrong town. The locals had heard of old Joe, seen the *Wanted* posters of the man with white eyes. They sprung a trap at the local honky-tonk. Lured him onto the dancefloor for line dancing. But those folks didn't form a line. They formed a circle, slowly closing in on Joe at the center. Once they'd thrown his body to the floor, the real dancing began. They crunched his bones under their boots. Gouged his white eyes with high heels. Stomped his flesh into mush. The dancefloor was coated in Cotton-Eyed Joe's blood as the townsfolk partied through the night. Come morning, they washed those hardwoods clean and brought what was left of the dead man to the pig farm for feeding. They all vowed to never speak of Cotton-Eyed Joe again. But someone did speak, and that person spoke to another person, until finally somebody wrote a song about him. Legend has it, if that song gets sung on the night he died, in the town where he was killed, Cotton-Eyed Joe will come back."

Emily yelped, dropping the burned-down cigarette that had just singed her finger. She'd been so wrapped up in the story, she forgot she was holding it.

Nita crossed her arms at Jonah. "And when did this killer dance party supposedly happen?"

"June 16th, 1971." Jonah looked up, hair parting to reveal his pale face. "In Ridgedale, Pennsylvania."

"Okay." Dylan clapped. "Good story, man. Love the *Sixth Sense* twist."

Cheers resonated through the gymnasium windows, and Emily seized the chance to say, "It sounds like the song is over. Can we all go back inside now?"

Spooked as she was, Emily was happy that Jonah followed them back into the school dance.

"Great dancing out there, everybody!" the DJ announced. "But it's time to turn down the tempo and find yourself a partner for this next tune."

The lights went red as the song from the *Armageddon* soundtrack kicked in. Jonah's story was scary, but not as scary to Emily as the dreaded slow dance.

She watched as Dylan and Nita paired off, as expected.

Less expected was Vicky Parsons tapping Robbie on the shoulder to say, "Dance with me." Robbie's jaw dropped as his dream girl dragged him out to the dance floor.

Emily hovered beside Jonah on the sidelines. Their eyes met for a breathless moment, then darted away.

"Um," he mumbled. "Would you ... maybe ... like to ..."

"I'd love to," she said, and took his hand.

They found their place in a sea of swaying students beneath the red lights. Emily wanted to remember this night and didn't want to miss a thing. She rested her head on Jonah's shoulder, wondering what magic the summer might hold. Maybe they'd be boyfriend and girlfriend by the time they were freshmen.

"I hope I didn't scare you," he said into her ear.

"No," she lied. "It was very creative. Mrs. Seitz would be proud. But where'd you hear that story?"

"I didn't hear the story." Jonah pulled away to look Emily in the eye. "I am the story."

"And I don't—"

The song cut mid-lyric and the lights clicked off.

Emily reached out blindly in the dark. "Jonah?"

The screaming began as an inhuman voice boomed over the speakers.

"WHERE DID YOU COME FROM?"

Strobe lights flashed as Emily tried to focus her vision. Students were still dancing around her, but they weren't slow dancing anymore. Their arms and legs thrashed violently, and every eye turned egg white. The possessed students punched and kicked at each other with relentless limbs while they cried out in pain.

"WHERE DID YOU GO?"

The strobe light died and all went quiet.

Emily trembled in the dark, still searching for ... "Jonah?"

A spotlight clicked on, shining down on the place where the boy once stood.

Only it wasn't Jonah standing there anymore.

"WHERE DID YOU COME FROM?"

It wasn't a black-skinned man or a white man covered in coal dust. The creature before her wasn't wearing skin at all. It was a seven-foot black void, imitating a human shape. Four long tentacles twitched faster than Emily could see, but her gaze was locked in on the bulbous head with eyes that weren't eyes. Just two endless holes filled with stringy white webs that sparkled and spun. Every thought fled Emily's brain as the black shape wrapped around her, pulling her close until her eyes pressed against the white abyss, showing her everything she never wanted to know.

"WHERE DID YOU GO?"

***

The police arrived at Ridgedale Middle School at 10:52 p.m. on June 19th, 2001.

The music had stopped. The lights were out. The gym floor was empty.

One hundred and fifty-seven 8th grade students disappeared that night, along with a half dozen teachers, leaving no trace in their wake.

They found only one survivor, hiding beneath the DJ booth. Curled into a ball with her hands covering her ears. Both eyes blinded with premature cataracts.

Emily Watkins was no longer a girl full of hope for the future.

She was a broken human record, spinning the same refrain for the rest of her days …

"Where did you come from, where did you go,

Where did you come from, where did you go,

Where did you come from, where did you go,

Where did you come from (Now jump at the person next to you and shout:)

COTTON-EYED JOE!"

Nostalgic Media Tells Us Where We've Been and Where We Are

Essay by Tiffany Morris

It's one of my earliest reading memories: chilling stories from classic authors, illustrations crosshatched with urgent depravity and strange beauty. *Mostly Ghostly: Eight Spooky Stories to Chill Your Bones* was a short, 56-page anthology of classic ghost stories adapted for young readers (9-12, though I was younger than nine when reading it). I didn't love it, necessarily, but it was designed to unnerve me and capture my attention all at once, and it did just that—haunting me and shaping my future writing career in the process.

It's kind of a funny juxtaposition for me in retrospect, to have been a quiet Mi'kmaw kid curled up in my unicorn-themed bedroom on a sunny afternoon, devouring tale after tale of terror written by authors from at least a century before. They almost certainly did not imagine me as their future audience at the time of writing, but, like so many others, I was paying close attention to the way terror can move through text, how the play between dread and the uncertain can be cathartic narrative territory, and how morbid fascination can hold a place in fiction over large swaths of time, crossing centuries and territories (both real and imaginal).

As an adult, getting into classic, the Gothic, and Weird literature has been its own reward, but one of the more amusing threads to me is the anxiety over property, estate land, and inheritance. As an Indigenous person and as an Eldest Millennial, I simply "Can't Relate" to the problem of not wanting an intruder in your manor grounds, a ghostly knight being a nuisance, or some such thing. These are good stories, to be sure, (and I detest the idea that a story must be relatable to be good) but it's still an observation that amuses me when I am delving into the adult versions of these genre anthologies.

Many of the stories in the *Mostly Ghostly* anthology stood out to me. Steve Zorn had picked a great selection between Edith Nesbit, Washington Irving, Ambrose Bierce, and others, but it was one story in particular that has stayed with me, the author's name burned into my memory as a reminder throughout the years: M.R. James, author of short stories like "Lost Hearts."

The anxiety in "Lost Hearts" has a hinge of inheritance, following an orphan sent to live on his uncle's estate, and learning some horrifying truths via ghostly apparitions along the way. Children's horror is inherently cosmic horror: the ordered world is unsteady and possibly malevolent, your reality and testimony is often questioned by others, and you are helpless to those more powerful than you, especially the sometimes anonymously powerful. "Lost Hearts" doesn't condescend to children about these fears, but leans into it, forming a world where the adults do not care about the wellbeing of their charge, and the relationships in it are increasingly found to be extractive, harmful, and endangering.

There is, too, a class component in this. Thankfully, Zorn excised some of the outdated xenophobic terminologies in the original story, but on reading the story as an adult, their inclusion only reinforces the disconnect between classes: the domestic worker, Mrs. Bunch, is a kindly class traitor who betrays the other marginalized characters in service of her wealthy boss. The story in both iterations demonstrates the extractive nature of relationships between the ultra-wealthy and the marginalized. This is especially apparent in cases where children have been abandoned to a bad fate. My story, "The Red Hourglass," picks up on this relationship dynamic and explores how our pain can and will be used against us, often in the name of healing offered at the hands of self-appointed, self-styled spiritual leaders. Increasingly, there is a wealth disparity in the healer and those seeking healing, whether it's a monetary expense or time expense that is prohibitive to access.

The evil uncle of "Lost Hearts" is using the occult to search for immortality. The search for immortality or eternal youth is exploitative in nature, and I wanted to include this idea of whole, healed perfection in this search. Brianna is slowly figuring out Elizabeth is a cult leader, and it becomes important for Brianna to try to escape her grasp. Brianna is only there because she'd been abandoned by her mother, another example of people finding and failing each other in vicious cycles of repeated violence (another aspect of "Lost Hearts").

The opposite of trauma, it's said, is play—so it's interesting to revisit nostalgic horror media and think about reading as play. Carrying this play element into creative works that explore trauma gives ample ground for how it is successfully integrated or resisted by characters. For Brianna to have the ending that she does was very important to me—to push against mass cultural narratives, that to heal one must give all of themselves, to dismantle and rebuild. In my experience, that dismantling, rebuilding, and integration comes anyway, especially if you are blessed with a favorite creative outlet, where certain characters are closer than they may appear.

Wela'lioq for reading!

THE RED HOURGLASS

BY TIFFANY MORRIS

Bright as a nuclear flash, Brianna thought, stepping out of the capsule. She closed her eyes and slowly blinked them back open as she adjusted to the light beyond the artificial metal womb. The city outside was rendered silent by the tempered glass. A little thrill ran over her cool smooth skin, beaded with salt water from the floatation tank. No one could see her staring down at them in the giant floor-to-ceiling windows. She was a looming naked angel gazing over the sprawl of buildings below, an impossible gargoyle, her own flesh perfect and strange in organic symmetry against the geometric perfection of the architecture. Every new city subdivision was like broken teeth that were capped in porcelain, the kind of teeth she dared to want someday, free of the evidence of her days of nicotine and coffee and weed. Who didn't want to pretend to have always been pure?

She toweled off in the softly-lit clinical space and pulled on a fuzzy white robe and sandals. Everything was doused in the rich scent of organic cleaning spray—some combination of lavender and mint, something meant to relax and revitalize while claiming to eliminate germs. Brianna breathed deeply of the smell, grateful for its simple luxury. Better than the antiseptic and vomit and soup smell of the hospital. She tied the robe tighter around her too-thin frame and walked out into the hushed quiet of the hall.

"Did you enjoy the saltwater re-story?" her Aunt Elizabeth asked, meeting her just outside the guest bedroom—one of five, Elizabeth had boasted, beaming. All occupied except the one that she had gotten a vision of, the one she'd known would be special; she had kept it empty after the last guest left last week. Then Brianna's message had come through—a plea for help from a long-lost relative. *I knew it*, Elizabeth had said in the car from the hospital. *I just knew it.*

"Yeah." Brianna nodded. "The session was … it was relaxing". She forced a quick smile to hide the crawl of irritation. Had Elizabeth been waiting for her, listening for her footsteps?

"Great! I always feel like I'm stepping out of the womb afterwards. Or like I'm out of a really hot shower."

"Yeah, it's womb-like for sure," Brianna said. Or so she guessed. She didn't remember being in the womb and didn't believe those whack jobs who claimed to remember it. The kind of people Elizabeth hung out with almost certainly made claims like that. Brianna's mother had always scoffed at her sister's eccentricities, her interest in the esoteric and the occult. Brianna didn't admit to her mother that she thought it was kind of cool, even though she maintained some of her own healthy skepticism on such matters.

It didn't matter what her mom thought anymore. Brianna had been blocked on all platforms after being discharged from the hospital. *Too much drama*, her mother always said, and she knew that this time she'd really meant it. Lucky that Aunt Elizabeth remembered her after ten years of distance and was thrilled to welcome her to the Lavender Healing Lodge, just outside the city, where beautiful glass buildings ate into the dusty rocks blasted out from the steep hills.

A muffled lullaby of music had played in the tank as the dark consumed her. Brianna had tried to turn off her brain—she assumed that was what you were supposed to do—and in those moments, let the world evaporate. Her body in the capsule, the capsule in the room, the room in the house, the house on the street, city, state, country, planet, galaxy—until everything that she knew existed only in the deep dark humming that thrummed beneath all things. But then she'd travelled back into herself, had seen herself at younger and younger ages, the clumsy fumble of her old selves, grasping forever at whatever she thought authenticity meant for her at the time. Scene upon scene of Brianna in the mirror, eyebrow furrowed with appraisal. Brianna knew her body's angles better than she knew anything about who she was: the sharpness of her hip bones, which she liked on her better days, on days she thought it contributed to a high fashion sort of gauntness, but her belly distended sometimes, and it bothered her, made her picture her skin tearing, thin tissue paper, and everything spilling out. When everyone else wore crop tops, she made sure to keep hidden.

"I'm sorry that I didn't know, you know, about how things have been for you," Elizabeth said. Her voice gentle as her grey eyes watered—

something of oysters and moonlight in them, similar to, but still different from, Brianna's own, the icy hues she inherited from her mother.

"It's okay," Brianna replied. She didn't know if it was supposed to be, but it's not like she had anywhere else to go.

"I'm here for you, whatever you need to share—or not. This is a healing place for all of us. It's not an even path for anyone."

"Thank you." It was all she could muster. Sometimes, people's sympathy for her felt like dissection. Brianna hated that feeling, her sadness catching her breath, a cracked rib, her stomach tissue knotted with dread like a skein of soaked yarn curling around her other organs, strangling her ability to process anything. This was why she never asked for help or offered it to others—the whole exchange was far too grotesque. There was only so much of another person's history she could handle—one of many reasons she didn't want to end up in a shelter or out on the street.

Elizabeth's eyes were on Brianna's bandaged wrist. Brianna hadn't realized she'd been picking at the gauze.

You're lucky to have survived it, the nurse had snapped at her, stitching up the sliced meat of her forearm.

"There's lemon water in the lounge," her aunt said. "Best to hydrate after time in the saltwater."

***

The lounge was bathed in deep silence. It was an almost artificial quiet, another womb space. Brianna looked around for signs that the space was soundproofed. She rubbed her palms against the textured wall, her hands traveling along the soft peach stucco. It was the house's rough skin, the only thing allowed to be imperfect and scarred. The fuzzy chairs looked and felt like bleached hair, and were miraculously unstained, shining in the sunlight. The whole room would probably glow rust-orange at sunset, a pristine desert oasis. Brianna grabbed a cup of water at the drink station, feeling the glass get colder as the water poured in a smooth stream.

A dead black widow spider sat atop the sour-bright yellow of the jar of lemon slices. It was bent at strange angles, an arachnid martyr in a museum painting. Brianna crushed it between her tattooed fingers, wondering where its poison was kept.

The red hourglass on its body crumpled into a heart. Lifeless black legs spasmed, then pulsated, before she flicked the evidence onto the perfect clean floor. Brianna wondered how often Elizabeth's maids came to clean each room. She picked up a book about chakras and the world slowly blurred into orbs of colored light.

***

Orange. Rust-blood smell and a stained scene, the pristine couches covered in arterial splatter. Brianna blinked her eyes again, over and over, trying to erase the room back into what it had been moments before, but the diseased dark tangled its hair on everything.

"Hello?" Brianna yelped. She shook her head. She'd fallen asleep and awakened at dusk—that was all, had to be all. She stood up and the floor met her and the rust taste poured into her throat. She gagged and dry heaved on the taste, the stale stench of a crime scene.

"Liz?" She managed to choke out. "Something's wrong."

Brianna pulled herself back up onto the couch. Her legs were half asleep, estranged from her body, marionette-limp.

"You're not going to be able to get out," a high, soft voice swam into her head. Had she heard it or imagined it?

"Hello?" Brianna screamed.

"Don't bother me with that," the voice said. "It won't help any."

Brianna managed to sit up on the couch and swiveled her neck to the corner where the voice was coming from. A figure was in deepest shadow in the corner.

"Are you a guest?" she asked. Even in this panic, a sheepish feeling of stupidity.

"Sort of," the voice said. "I apologize, but I can only hear you. I think I've gone blind. I'm all bandaged up and healing."

"Why can't I—why can't we—leave?"

"The door's locked," the voice said simply.

"Were you here this whole time?"

Silence.

"Hello?"

"I don't think here is where you think it is," the voice finally responded. "I heard you get wheeled in."

Brianna's head swam again. Her phone. She fumbled in her pocket. Empty. This was the same trapped insect feeling she'd had in the hospital. Maybe she was dreaming. Maybe she had dreamed the visit to Elizabeth and was now in a nightmare absorbing the sounds and psychic energies of the hospital.

She slapped herself on the face, a hot feeling of each finger pressed into her cheeks, her smooth face skin. Her right hand, of course—the left was still weak, wrist covered in gauze.

"I need to wake up," she muttered.

"I don't think you're asleep," the voice said.

"Show me your face," Brianna demanded. "Show me your face. I'm tired of just hearing your commentary."

Hesitation wasn't a sound, but an energy. Then a rustle of movement, a shuffle of feet, the slow emerging of discernible features as she encountered the constantly dimming light—a short woman, shoulders slightly hunched, her entire face wrapped in layers of bandage. The eye sockets were bled through, small indentations oozing blood and pus.

"You—you have an infection," Brianna breathed. She hoped she disguised the gag scratching her uvula, the scream wrestling its way up from her gut.

"She hasn't come to change my gauze," the woman whimpered. "I've lost track of time."

"Who? Elizabeth?"

Silence, then, finally, a nod.

The barbed-wire snarl of the still-healing scar in her wrist ached. Brianna wanted to scream with her whole being, to let the anguish wash the room in another dark. She punched at her legs. The hot anthill pain of sensation returned to them, crawling and spasming upward from her feet.

"Can you try the door?" Brianna asked.

"I heard her lock it when you came in."

"Okay," Brianna said, locking her eyes on the window. "I'll go out the window and I'll send help back for you."

"I don't need help," the voice said. "Or I do, but that's why I'm here." A pause. "Isn't that why you're here?"

"No," Brianna said. "Not this kind of help."

"You should stay," the woman shrilled, her voice edged with hysteria, nearing a shriek. "She'll help you; she's helping all of us."

Brianna stood. Pain shot up through her calves, but she was steady enough to walk. To run. She ignored the woman and pressed her palms against the window, feeling around for an opening. There was none, of course: the windows didn't open.

She took a deep breath of metallic air. Brianna punched the glass with her right hand, ignoring as best she could the pain of the impact, the echo of the pain as she repeated the motion over and over, the crack that surrendered thunderous then shattered into a rainfall of glass as her rage opened the portal of the window and she managed to pull her small body through it, tattoo writing on her hands rendered indiscernible with blood and shadow as she pushed her way out into the sharp night of red dust and glass buildings, everything shining as she ran on awakening legs deeper into the uncertainty of the city still awaiting her.

***

When she learned of the cult activity of the Lavender Healing Lodge, its leader found years later with her eyes cut out in a ritual of ascension, Brianna was happy to have foregone any perfection, any promise of rebirth. She had run into the snaking spine of herself and found a nest of black widows there. They waited with their hourglass poisons, ready to pour out and puncture deserving skin.

FILM AND TELEVISION: FLICKERING LIGHTS IN THE DARK

Haunted VHS tapes, late-night cable access television and enigmatic horror hosts. In this section we explore our relationship with television and film, and how the small and silver screen has influenced our love of horror.

Lights Out

by Diane Funston

11:30 Saturday nights, after the local news,
Gregory the Grave Walker, hiking through
the cemetery with his jagged cane,
would enter our small living room.

Lights out, except for the glow of the TV,
my mother asleep in her bedroom,
Uncle Lou and I in our weekly communion
of English muffin pizzas and fear.

Black-and-white classics: wolf-men
who only changed at full moon;
vampires, who would sacrifice
even the innocent for their drink;
man-made monsters, sorriest lot of them all,
despised by a society
that did too little, too late.

My teenage Saturday nights,
Uncle Lou, in his forties,
we walked with Gregory,
a double feature.

Afterward, I'd steady Lou to his feet,
he'd stagger to his bedroom, and I'd make sure
his cigarette was out, that he'd taken his meds,
that I tossed his beer bottles into the trash.
I'd turn the TV off then, just in time
to catch Gregory laugh his last evil laugh.

THE TALE OF THE GIRL WHO LOVED HORROR MOVIES

ESSAY BY EMILY RUTH VERONA

I can still hear the theme song. The flutter of disembodied laughter. As a kid, I felt brave watching *Are You Afraid of the Dark?* all alone in my room—as if it proved something. I grew up with siblings a decade older than me, with a brother who listened to Metallica late into the night and who showed me horror movies I was too young to watch. Should I have seen the unrated *Spawn* VHS when I was eight? No. Did I? Of course I did.

Watching *Are You Afraid of the Dark?* was different than being handed my brother and sister's movies, though. It was *mine*. I discovered it on my own and staying up late to watch it felt very grown-up at the time. It was the last kids show of the night before *The Brady Bunch* and *I Love Lucy* came on. This was almost like a stepping stone: the bridge between my world and one of more adult stories.

Are You Afraid of the Dark? combined a heady blend of '90s nostalgia with a spine-tingling spookiness that still holds up today, even in the show's silliest episodes. It's what made me want to read about witchcraft and place recording devices in empty rooms hoping to catch the sound of ghosts whispering from the walls. I didn't read much horror as a child, despite being an avid reader. I was bewitched by the *Dear America* book series, loving anything and everything centered on historical fiction—but I also watched a ton of *Are You Afraid of the Dark?* and this left an indelible mark on my imagination.

As I got a little older, my fascination with scary stories grew. I started watching contemporary horror movies on my own, convincing my friends to watch them with me whenever I could. *Scream. Final Destination. Thirteen Ghosts. Sleepy Hollow.* I became an avid movie nerd and horror fan. I can still remember the thrill I felt watching the *Final Destination 2* trailer for the first time. I was the kid who brought her own DVD of the movie *Saw* to a middle school sleepover. I was the girl who awaited her seventh day after watching *The Ring* with bated breath.

Even as a love of horror became a tacit facet of my personality, history remained one of my favorite subjects. I was particularly drawn to dark histories and I don't think it was a surprise to anyone when my interest in horror and my interest in history began to bleed into one another. Nothing thrilled me like a good horror film set in the past. *The Others* was definitely one of my early favorites, but I was just as fascinated by horror films made in the past. I dug into classics like *Psycho, Halloween, Rope,* and *Mystery of the Wax Museum.* I learned the histories behind the movies, keenly fascinated by "cursed" movie set stories that blossomed from Hollywood lore about *Poltergeist* and *The Exorcist.*

With so many movies to watch and histories to learn, *Are You Afraid of the Dark?* fell to the wayside during my teenage years. This was in the days before streaming services, and when Nickelodeon stopped airing the episodes I ceased to have access to them. I continued to remember the show fondly, but thought about it less and less as the years went on.

Cue college. It turns out that the very first friend I made on campus during orientation had also grown up watching *Are You Afraid of the Dark?*—and she was a Creative Writing major, just like me. We soon bonded over a shared love for this strange and unusual children's series. I found out that she had a bunch of episodes recorded onto a VHS when she was a kid and had since transferred those episodes onto a flash drive, complete with original '90s commercials, which were sometimes terrifying in their own right and for all the wrong reasons.

We began to spend our Friday nights ordering Chinese food and watching old episodes of *Are You Afraid of the Dark?* on her laptop. It was nostalgic in a way I had never experienced before because this was a show I had never shared with anyone. Of course, not all of the episodes were as scary as we remembered, but some held up shockingly well. "The Tale of Laughing in the Dark" (season one, episode two), for instance, is packed with dread—and cigar smoke. The practical monster effects for "The Tale of Dead Man's Float" (season five, episode one) look even better today than a lot of CGI monsters in more contemporary R-rated films—and I've certainly watched enough of them to know.

To this day, the two of us will still have virtual *Are You Afraid of the Dark?* watch parties, though we haven't had one in quite some time. Life happens. People get busy. I published a book and started dating the person who would turn out to be the love of my life. She got engaged to her girlfriend and just recently acquired an agent for her middle grade novel. We don't talk as much as we used to but I know that anytime one of us needs it, the other will be ready for an *Are You Afraid of the Dark?* marathon. No questions asked. The show bonded us and has become an unexpected throughline across our friendship.

Horror as a genre has given me so much personally, culturally, and professionally. My debut thriller *Midnight on Beacon Street* (published by Harper Perennial in early 2024) is about a teenage babysitter who loves horror movies. This genre is nostalgic for me because it has remained a true, unwavering constant. There's not a corner of my life this genre has not touched. Some people might find it strange—taking comfort in the familiarity of the macabre. But those who love the genre know the comfort, and the community, to be found there. We like to be afraid of the dark.

LAST SHOW OF THE NIGHT

BY EMILY RUTH VERONA

You're nine years old and you're sitting up in bed. Shoulders hunched forward. Fists balling up the comforter. Your brother's old television set, the 13" x 13" box with plastic panels on the sides made to look like wood, is now in your room. It only took a little bit of begging, and the promise to your parents that you won't leave it on all weekend. It's the last kids' show of the night before the station switches to family sitcom reruns from the 1960s. You were going to turn the lights off, but decided against it—because you know better than to sit in the dark.

The opening theme sends a prickle down your arms like spider legs racing. The tilted close-ups transfix you. An empty swing. An attic door. A puppet's smiling face. Your breath hitches in your throat. What will it be tonight? Young campers lost in the woods? An abandoned swimming pool with a dark secret lurking beneath its depths? A magic shop where the magic is real, but at a terrible price? Mist drifts across the screen and you can feel the cool lick of it on the back of your neck.

The bedroom around you begins to fade away, blurring at the edges of your vision as the television welcomes you into a shining, sunny afternoon on a quiet, tree-lined street. The stories always start the same, with a bright, comforting soundtrack and familiar setting. The streets are a little cleaner, the yards more evenly mowed, and the houses bigger—but the street coming into a close-up right now, it looks just like your street. Just like any street you've ever been on. And that's what the show wants: for you to feel safe.

There is a light-blue house on the corner with a little girl standing in the driveway. You see much of yourself in the way she wears a flannel shirt tied around her waist, the backwards baseball cap on her head. The one that belonged to her brother. But he's off at college and she's all alone now—all alone in their new house down the street from an old cemetery. That's how their mom got such a good deal on the place—who would want to live next to a graveyard?

The little girl reminds you so much of yourself that you can't remember the name her mother calls to her from the garage as she unpacks. So you give her your name in your head. The little girl who is you but not you is desperate to make friends in this new town, but it's August. School hasn't started yet and no other kids live on the graveyard street. As the days stretch on, the little girl starts to take long walks all around the neighborhood just to pass the time.

At first, she stays away from the cemetery—with its tall, itchy grass and big iron gate. It's like something out of a movie—in fact, you're pretty sure you've seen this exact gate in a movie before. You can't remember the title, but it was one of those scary movies your brother said not to tell your mom about.

The little girl who is you but not you walks by this gate every day until, eventually, boredom gets the better of her. She decides to take a look inside. At least in the cemetery, she isn't alone. Not really.

Her mom works all the time, and doesn't notice when her daughter begins to spend whole afternoons talking to headstones. The headstones always listen, never interrupt her or ignore what she's saying by talking about something else. The little girl likes to call each headstone by name. She wonders what kind of lives the people buried beneath them must have lived.

There is one headstone in particular that she likes to sit by—that of a boy who had been about her own age, born a century ago into a much different world. The engraving doesn't say how the boy died, but it must have been tragic. A child's death is never anything but tragic. The little girl wonders if death is a lonely place, if the little boy enjoys her visits.

The cemetery becomes a haven. The only place in town where she feels like she can be herself. One day the little girl, assuming the boy she visits must have once lived here, asks the headstone if he had a favorite spot to go when he felt lonely.

"You wouldn't like it," comes the reply.

You jump in your seat and the little girl spins around to see a pretty boy with blue eyes. He looks to be about her own age, but his clothes are old—his white shirt baggy and frayed. The girl doesn't seem to notice that part but you do right away.

You and the girl stare wide-eyed at the boy, mouths ajar. "What wouldn't I like?" she asks.

He shrugs, hands in his pockets as he looks down at the grass. "The bell tower," he replies. He's got freckles and thick hair that makes you and the girl blush. "It's at the top of the church on Main Street. You can see all the way to the mountains from there."

The little girl knows the church he's talking about—it's old, closed now with boarded up windows. It has a tall, pointed steeple that shoots straight up at the sky. "Why wouldn't I like it?"

"It's pretty high up," he says. "And the bell rings on the hour every hour. At least, it used to."

"I'm not scared of heights," says the little girl, even though you both know it's a lie. She is afraid of heights and you are too. She looks out across the graveyard in the direction of town and the church bell, but when she turns back to ask the boy another question, he is gone.

For days the girl who is you but not you thinks about the bell, about what the boy said. She starts taking walks into town—even though she's not supposed to go that far by herself—just to stare at the bell tower. Every time it looks even taller, more imposing. Her palms sweat. You can feel the clamminess in your hands.

On her third day of walking into town, the little girl circles the church and manages to find one window in the back of the building where a board has been pried away. The space is small but not so small that she can't climb through it and so she does, even though every muscle in her body is aching for her to stop—to go back.

Inside, the church is quiet and dark. None of the lights are on and all the pews have a fine layer of dust on them that tickles at the girl's nose. But the walls look sturdy, the floorboards strong. The little girl takes a step, half-expecting the place to collapse around her—and when it doesn't, she takes another.

She finds the stairs to the bell tower in the far corner of the nave— she does not know the nave is what the main room of a church is called, but you do. She takes those stairs all the way to the top. It's a long, winding walk. The stairway would be pitch black but there's a stained glass window near the second floor landing that lets in a soft rush of rainbow-colored light. The girl climbs the stairs all the way to the top, and when she gets there she sees a big bronze bell centered at the top of the steeple. The bell is roughly the size of the shed in her backyard, with ropes and gears all around it. Like the pews, everything up here is covered in dust. There are only three walls up in the steeple, a big open space gaping where a fourth would be. She takes a step forward into the fresh air. The boy was right, you can see the whole town from this height—all the way beyond the forest and across the hills. She takes another step toward the edge and your hands dig into the sides of the bed, the balled-up comforter squeezed between your palms. She is going too far out. She should turn back.

Another step. Your hands squeeze tighter. What is she doing? Your brain is screaming for her to stop—to get away from the edge! *Look out! Look out! Look out!*

Suddenly, an old man grabs the girl by the shoulder and spins her around. At first, he looks like a ghost—but his clothes aren't old-timey. He's wearing a pair of grease-stained jeans and a blue T-shirt with a toolbelt around his waist. "What are you doing up here?" he shouts, shaking her. "Don't you know it's dangerous?"

The actor playing the old man is over-the-top and cartoonish, but your heart is pounding all the same.

"I just—I just wanted to see the view," the girl stammers.

"You've got to be careful," he says gruffly, pulling her by the arm back toward the stairs. "You know a little boy fell from that tower and died! That's why it's off-limits!" He drags her downstairs and out the door, which as some kind of caretaker or handyman he seemed to have had the key to open, and the little girl begs him not to call her mother. He agrees, reluctantly, so long as she promises not to come back.

The little girl should run all the way home. It's getting dark, she's feeling shaky, but instead she heads to the cemetery. The little boy is waiting for her next to her favorite headstone. She's angry and her cheeks are flushed. You feel her anger circulating through your own body. "Why did you tell me to go there?"

The boy's face sours. He says nothing.

"You're him!" she shouts. "You're the boy who fell from the tower! Why did you send me there? No one is supposed to be up there! I got in trouble!"

At last, he looks up at her. "I'm lonely."

The girl's mouth is half-open, but the words don't come. Because she understands. She doesn't want to be lonely either. But sometimes you don't get to choose. Loneliness doesn't ask for permission. And so she makes a deal with the boy. She agrees to visit his grave after school when she can—to talk to him and tell him stories so that neither of them are lonely ever again.

It's a sweet ending. Not all the episodes of this show have nice endings, but this one was sweet. Only, your heart is still hammering. Because you don't trust the boy. No matter what he said. No matter how the episode closed. He will try again. Maybe not the next day or the day after that, but eventually he will try. Even if the little girl who is you but not you can't see that. A pit swells in your stomach. The dead always try again. They can't help it.

Your brother certainly can't.

He's been gone for a year now and every night he stands in the corner of your room. Waiting. Watching. He's lonely and he wants you to join him, to go down to the basement where he had his accident and find the way to him. But you know better than to listen. Because the dead aren't the same as they were when they were living. They're different. They change. Your brother is no longer your brother. But you have his TV. And his hat. And your memories. They are more important than the shadow in the corner of your room. They are what's real.

Your firsts squeeze even tighter at your sides as the credits for the TV show begin to roll. When you lift up your hands, you're holding fistfuls of graveyard dirt.

Bodies up the Wall

by L. Stephenson

He dragged her up the wall. Oh god, he dragged her up the wall.

Her body leaves a trail, like a paint roller made of meat. A path of smeared blood on paper, scrolling, leading to her demise.

She screams for her lover.

She clutches her bloodied breast.

And then she falls.

Glistening red erupts from her sheets, like a large stone cast into a silent pond.

Run! my mind cries. *Run! Run! Run!*

I scream my way through the house, a banshee of tears and fear. I take refuge, cowering in the dining room.

Don't let Freddy get me …

Waiting to Be Born: Watching *Night Gallery*

Essay by Jan Stinchcomb

I grew up keeping family secrets and consoling myself with books, movies, and television. *Night Gallery* scared me with its theme song alone, though I was a kid who didn't scare easily. Once I got past the disturbing music of the *Night Gallery* series, I could sink into each episode, many of which were taken from famous short stories. Two of them featured child characters who reached out to me.

"The Doll," based on a 1946 Algernon Blackwood story, features a revenge plot, a lovely English girl, and a frightening doll with black-ringed eyes and poisonous teeth. The doll arrives in a box sent to the Devonshire household of a certain Colonel Masters, who once ordered the execution of an Indian rebel in Hyderabad. Monica, his niece and ward, falls in love with the doll and refuses to part with it. "She's very sweet. And very bright too. She can talk and sing and do all sorts of things," she declares to her baffled uncle and governess.

Each shot of the doll, with her vicious smile and wild eyes, terrified me. Despite the doll's capacity for violence—we see what happens to her competition, a pretty doll she immediately quarters and disembowels—Monica is not afraid of it. Her loyalty and affection never waver, and she is quick to convey the conversations she has with her new friend: "She talks to me about all kinds of things, especially you. She must be very fond of you, Uncle. She's always mentioning your name." Monica's lack of fear, her willingness to cuddle this veritable Halloween prop, fascinated me as a child. Why isn't she afraid of those sharp white teeth?

We learn the doll is a gift from the brother of the man Colonel Masters executed back in Hyderabad. Shortly thereafter, the doll completes her mission, killing the colonel with one lethal bite. Masters cannot outrun his colonial misdeeds, though he does arrange to have his own murderous doll sent to his enemy, thus perpetuating the cycle of magic.

Masters is dead, the doll is thrown on the fire, and Monica survives. Should I have taken Monica as my role model? Her relationship with the deadly doll gives her some measure of power. She is not only unafraid of evil but is its willing servant while it dwells in her household. My family excelled at denying the reality of mental illness and abuse. Were they merely coping, or were they, like Monica, under a spell? In my own writing I have returned to the issue of intergenerational trauma and decided that it is better, both in life and in art, to wake up from the spell.

Another *Night Gallery* episode that deals with the sudden appearance of a magical entity in the life of a child is "Brenda," but this time the lonely girl refuses to let go of her new friend. Brenda is socially awkward and a bully, bored and isolated on the small island where her family is vacationing. Her father isn't sure what to do with her, but he does lecture her on ethics and the importance of making good choices.

After finding a big hairy creature in the woods, one who is more comical than frightening, Brenda traps it in a hole referred to as "the old pit." She talks to it, speculating about its age and how it came to be on the island. The most interesting thing to come out of their one-way conversation is an especially poignant question. "Do you want to be born?" Brenda asks. This inquiry, an expression of yearning, is at the heart of the episode and central to the 1954 Margaret St. Clair story on which it is based.

Brenda coaxes the creature out of the hole but runs off before it fully emerges. Later that night she leaves the door to her house open, and the creature enters. Her panicked parents and the other adults of the community rush to contain the creature, ultimately imprisoning it in the old pit, which they fill with rocks. Brenda is devastated when she learns her family is leaving the island early. The reaction of the adults, especially of her father, is puzzling. They can't kill the creature, as it is impervious to bullets, and so they resign themselves to containment and secrecy. Her father refuses to discuss the creature with Brenda, and both her parents believe she would not be able to survive the sight of it. Like Monica, though, Brenda has already begun to commune with this unnamable force which so terrifies the adults in her life.

She comes back to the island the next year and is relieved to hear a growl from within the pile of rocks. Her final words are heartbreaking: "I love you. I'll always love you. You're the only one I could ever love. But I'll let you out, I promise. I'll give you life. I'll give you love. Oh, yes. Oh, yes. We'll be born together. We'll be born, you and I, together."

So what is this thing the adults must destroy, this only love of a desperately lonely girl? Is it simply the dangerous outside world or is it something more specific, like sexuality? Is it Brenda's true self? Perhaps originality is the biggest threat to Brenda's community, which is both wealthy and conventional. A refusal to conform to family and society, as evidenced even more strongly in the St. Clair story, may be the real monster.

Horror taps into that which we cannot name, but which threatens us all the same. But for those of us drawn to the weird and uncanny, it also provides a home. I still turn on the television when I can't sleep at night. I look for allies, other people who are not so much refusing to grow up as waiting for their moment to be born.

Twist Your Back

by Jillian Bost

Sarah trembled in her frigid January room, doom in her belly as she willed herself to forget the twisted spine, the manic cackle, and the choking, skeletal face.

Zelda.

A being forged by death in a twisted ruin of hatred and despair.

"She's gonna get you, Sarah," her brother taunted. "She's gonna come out of the TV and twist your back. You'll never get out of bed again!"

Movies couldn't scare her; she was too old. She knew about actors. Special effects. Scripts.

But she lay on her little bed of springs and mothball linen, and dreamed of antiseptic agony.

THE ART OF HORROR: SUBLIMINAL TERRORS INSPIRED BY MUSIC, ILLUSTRATION AND THE VISUAL ARTS

Ghastly images, haunting paintings and eerie illustrations have captured the imagination of countless horror lovers throughout time. This section explores how the visual, musical, and performing arts influenced our love of horror in the most delicious way.

SUBMECHANOPHOBIA

BY ERIN JO ELDRY

Man-made objects submerged in water
Yearn to be feared in that place where they don't belong

Under the cover of my hands, I don't want to look
Not at that sea serpent made of Lego in Orlando
Deathly afraid in the cinema of the luxury liner sinking in the ocean
Everyone else in the meanwhile cry over Jack and Rose
Reruns on television, the likes of *Sphere*, *The Deep*, and *Jaws*
Watching with racing heart the swimming pool episode of *Are You Afraid of the Dark?*
Am I scared of the so-called animals that lurk along the Jungle Cruise?
That's a nonsensical question, of course I am terrified
Entering the propeller room of the ghost ship, Queen Mary
Runs a chill through me, more so than the spirits

Now that I have a word for it
It's interesting how willingly I go looking
Going out of my way to seek what lurks in the water
Happy to observe it, unscathed, and kind of charmed
Take me with you if you go diving
Many of the findings give me such a tingle
A courageous swell in the heart
Replacing that shy and nervous shiver
Especially now that I am older

SHADES OF HORROR

ESSAY BY R.J. JOSEPH

Nothing could beat the thrill I felt watching classic horror movies on Saturday mornings and afternoons. Since I was born in the seventies, many of the features were in black and white and had been made anywhere from the 1920s up to that glorious time of disco, sideburns, and bell bottoms. The starkness of shading, rather than color, brought a certain broodiness to films from those times. Viewers were prompted to use their own devices to make determinations of monstrosity and horror. The shadowed darkness prevailed over the random bright reveals to display the flexibility of shades. Of nuance, if you will.

These spaces between the shadows are where I loved to investigate and pursue questioning about the stories. I wanted to know what was happening in the dark parts of the story; in the murky crevices inside the human psyche where all we could see were shades of gray rather than stark black or white. The monsters weren't all good or all bad. They were nuanced. The protagonists didn't always have the best of intentions because they showed up in shading too.

Creatures displayed in the films were designed with darker shades, allowing them to hide in the shadows when they wanted to, which startled viewers when they appeared in the bright light of day. We could clearly see that which we were supposed to be frightened by. However, the most frightening monsters were those who could be well camouflaged in daytime, such as the impostors in *Invasion of the Body Snatchers* (1956). We understood they were worthy adversaries in the dark, because we saw their major activity happening then. Once they moved operations to the day, we understood humanity was in far more danger than we could have imagined.

In these classics, a character that had dark hair was also typically cast as the antagonist. Their brunette tresses served as dark helmets of depravity, or at the very least, unladylike desires and motivations. Light-colored hair was reserved for victims or protagonists the audience was supposed to root for, to want to persevere over the evil that threatened them. Darker clothing and hair shades were reserved for aged women in these movies, such as those worn by the character Blanche Hudson (Joan Crawford) in *What Ever Happened to Baby Jane?* (1962). Her nemesis, Baby Jane Hudson (Bette Davis) donned the lighter-colored clothing and hair typically reserved for youth—and innocence.

My favorite thing about these classic black-and-white horror films was how displaying the story in shades allowed for this switching of archetypes. When the villain was displayed in light and sunshine, the level of monstrosity became elevated. Patty McCormack gave one of my favorite monstrous performances as a cute little murderous blonde girl, Rhoda Penmark, in *The Bad Seed* (1956). Janet Leigh later gave us the sultry, blonde Marion Crane in *Psycho* (1960) who had done a terrible deed, but didn't necessarily deserve the vicious murder delivered to her by "Mother." But, of course, we had sympathy for the light Crane as she was attacked by the shadowy "Mother" who relied on those shades to hide her true identity.

Shadows are spooky and chilling, but they can also be comforting. They appear when there is a light source somewhere to create them, so they exist in a dichotomous relationship with that which can be seen. Creating monsters and characters in shades of black, white, and gray gives the characters places to hide, whether in darkness or in the light. These shades of horror provide space for me to create characters with nuance, with their own shadows, so readers can decide for themselves who they will root for.

I'm always rooting for the shades of horror.

PritTee

by R.J. Joseph

Thalia tried her hardest to keep her face straight and eyes forward as her mother preached to her—again. Any shift from deference would make the litany go on that much longer.

"I buy you this stuff and you always lose it. Money just going down the drain for nothing. We don't have money like that to waste on frivolous things." She put her hands on her hips. Then she sighed, the long, deep mournful cry of the always put upon. "But Lord knows I want you to be more ladylike so folks will know you're a girl and not some thrown away child."

Thalia thought she would bust from standing so still for so long. But she really wanted to get her nails done, so she had to be really, really respectful and appear to be contrite. She started counting inside her head to help the time pass.

Finally, her mother threw her hands up in the air. "You know what? Fine. *Fine.* I'll let you go to the nail shop." She searched around the kitchen for her purse.

When she found it, she held bills out in her hand toward her daughter. As the girl reached out for the money, her mother used her free hand to point and punctuate her warnings.

"Go straight there and come straight back. No talking to those boys on the corner. And when you get to the shop, tell them you only want the shellac on your natural nails. No powder or tips." She handed Thalia the money.

"And no fast colors like red or hot pink."

"Yes, ma'am."

The older woman narrowed her eyes. "I mean it."

"Yes, ma'am," Thalia repeated. "Thank you," she added emphatically so her mother wouldn't take her respectfulness as ambivalence. She needed Mama to know she was super excited to get her nails done and she appreciated that she was finally allowed to do it.

Thalia almost skipped to the corner nail shop, stopping only when she remembered sixteen-year-olds weren't supposed to skip like little kids. She settled, instead, on a brisk walk with her arms to her sides.

The change in her gait wasn't enough to keep the boys and old men on the opposite corner from whistling at her and trying to get her attention. She ignored them and didn't even get mad like she usually did. Her steps faltered as she instantly wondered if getting her nails done would make them bother her even more.

She didn't have the curves most of her classmates had, and she still wore training bras a lot of times. She stayed dressed in ragged jeans and vintage rapper tee shirts, and she wore no makeup. She felt she was built like a 2 x 4, not too tall, and straight up and down, front and back.

None of that stopped those men. She hoped new polish wouldn't serve as an evolution of her status, an invitation for them to harass her into oblivion. She hated the attention and it felt creepy. It *was* creepy.

She didn't like to try pretty things for them, or even the boys at her school. Unlike the dirty old men in the neighborhood, the boys at school treated her like she was invisible. She was such a nonentity to them that she sometimes had to pinch herself to make sure she was real.

She didn't want to try pretties for the other girls, either. So many of them went overboard with the embellishments, wearing expensive designer clothing that Thalia never even heard of. She thought it was cool that they wore full makeup to school, and it got them the attention they said they wanted. Good for them, really—especially if they got pretty just because it made them feel good.

Thalia wasn't there where they were. She just wanted to learn who she was and how she felt best. Sure, one day, she would probably want attention from somebody. But for the current time, she just wanted to feel good in her own skin, with whatever clothing and accessories she might want to add.

As the manicurist worked to put on the prettiest shade of light blue Thalia had ever seen, the girl thought about the stuff Mama was already fussing about. Thalia had asked for a pastel turquoise, women's cut tee shirt she thought she might like. She put it on, and the color washed out her skin and made her bare face look sickly. The lace along the sleeves made the shirt look almost like a costume.

She took the shirt and wadded it up, then placed it in the back corner of her closet, where her mother rarely went.

The shirt wasn't what Mama was talking about since she still didn't realize Thalia never wore it. She was talking about the satin hair bonnet Thalia had begged for when she was sure it would help tame her kinky coily hair while she slept at night. Mama had insisted she only needed the cheap bandanas she had always supplied, but Thalia stood firm on wanting the bonnet. Then she only wore it twice. On the third morning, she couldn't find where it landed after it apparently slid from her head.

Once she gave up looking for it, and thought her mother may have forgotten about it, she asked for an assortment of colored hair scrunchies to wear her hair up and back in ponytails. Her mother gave her a side-eye, but said nothing else as she asked which colors.

"You pick, Mama," Thalia could warm her mother up when she had to. "You know best."

That little bit of charm worked, and Thalia got her scrunchies, many more than she'd hoped for. They had come in all sorts of colors, too: pastels, neons, jewel tones, metallic. And them being as vibrant as they were, they still quickly became invisible. They disappeared by the handful until Thalia could only find a few of them. During the time she half-heartedly searched for them, she decided she actually didn't care to wear her hair up or back very often, after all. The only reason she continued to look for them on occasion was just in case Mama remembered she hadn't seen them and Thalia needed to show proof she hadn't wasted or destroyed them.

The manicure was different. This was a big move and Thalia kept her promise to keep up the color, smiling every time she passed her mother in the house, and she stared to make sure the blue was still on. Thalia used these encounters to purposely showcase her nails, grabbing items, or posing with her hands up on the wall, bright nails sparkling in the light. Her mother would laugh at her obvious attempts to show off her nails, and after two weeks, she stopped looking, satisfied Thalia was keeping her word.

One morning at the start of the third week, Thalia woke up to see small flakes of light blue, still holding the shape of her fingernails, lying on her bed next to her pillow. Her right thumb burned at the tip, and she examined it to try to see why it hurt. She couldn't figure out how she'd taken the shellac off intact like that.

She decided she must have done it with her teeth, biting her thumb in the process. She sucked her thumb and gathered the flakes up to put them in the wastebasket, where Mama might not find them. With her thumb in her mouth, she went down for breakfast.

"Thalia! Why do you have your thumb in your mouth? You shouldn't eat that stuff." She noticed Thalia's bare nails and sucked her teeth.

Thalia waited for the anger she was sure would come. And she waited. Waited longer. Finally, her mother sighed.

"At least you kept them on for a full two weeks. That's about how long they're supposed to last, anyway."

Thalia released the breath she had been holding. When her mother smiled, Thalia offered a small grin of her own in return.

"You'll have to wait till payday next week before you go get them done again."

"Yes, ma'am."

"And stop chewing on that thumb so it won't be sore when you go back to the nail shop."

"Yes, Mama." Thalia ate her breakfast slowly, relishing the olive branch her mother had offered, hanging in the atmosphere.

Thalia's mood was still light when she went to bed that night. Despite her mood assuring that she'd have sweet dreams, she awoke sharply to the loud sound of rustling. She peered around her room in the darkness, trying to focus on where the noise came from.

She fumbled for her phone and turned on the flashlight.

When it landed in the corner next to her bed, she caught a flurry of movement.

Standing next to the wastebasket was a small body that sort of reminded her of the pictures of raccoons she saw on television.

But it was no raccoon. Its body was covered in scales with tufts of hair breaking through the plates. It stood over the wastebasket, but it wasn't tall enough to reach into it without the loud rustling through the contents Thalia had heard.

Most of the tufts had colorful scrunchies on them, twisted tightly—probably so they wouldn't come off. On the creature's head lay Thalia's lost bonnet, rolled up to better fit the small skull. Two wide eyes, set inside a large face covered with more tufts of hair focused on Thalia.

The creature held up Thalia's discarded tee shirt as a skirt, with one appendage that looked like a foot, but with more digits. On three of the digits lay the blue shellac Thalia had put in the wastebasket earlier.

"Prit. Tee." The raspy word came from the slit in its face.

Thalia stared, silent.

The creature spoke again, holding its appendage toward the girl. Its eyes held a plea.

"Prit. Tee."

The blue shellac slid off the—toes? Fingers?— and Thalia could feel the frustration coming from the small body.

She thought for a moment and then spoke softly. "Maybe I can help you with some glue."

The creature kept large eyes on Thalia as the girl moved slowly toward her desk drawer on the other side of the bed.

She returned with a bottle of glue and motioned for the shellac. Once she put a drop of glue on it, she pressed it on and put the creature's other appendage over it to hold it.

She repeated the motion with the other pieces of shellac. She ran out before she could cover each of the fingernail shaped scales at the tips of them.

The creature began to tremble and looked woefully at the ones that remained naked.

"I have something that might help a little." Thalia returned to her desk and picked up a blue marker. The shade wasn't a match, but it was still colorful.

She used it to cover the remaining tips. As she worked, the hairs on the creature began to sway and dance within the bounds of the scrunchies.

"Prit. Tee. Prit. Tee." The creature crooned and danced with the new color. The tee shirt swirled around the floor like the fanciest ball gown.

Thalia raised her finger to her mouth, with a shushing motion. "Please don't wake my mama up."

PritTee gazed at her and danced toward the closet.

"I can do an even better job tomorrow if you come back." Thalia felt a kinship with the creature, who also just wanted to be pretty. They could experiment together. With a wave, the creature disappeared back into the night.

The next morning, Thalia told her mother she'd changed her mind about getting her nails done again. "I think I might be able to do better with nail polishes here at home."

Her mother weighed her words. "That would be cheaper. I could bring you a few bottles of polish home with me this evening. Any special colors you want? No red or hot pink."

Thalia smiled at her mother. "One turquoise, please. But the rest, you pick, Mama. You know best."

RACKHAM'S TREE

ESSAY BY DARREN CROUCHER

Arthur Rackham's illustrations, eldritch and beautiful, haunting and mesmerizing, whole worlds of sprites and creatures and darkness slithering around the twisted trees and through the dying skies. Tattered clouds rushing like flesh torn away, leaving only hollow bones. In his hands *The Wind In The Willows* became a phantasmagoria. The piper at the gates of dawn heralding safety from the shadows hunting through the dark, dense forest where trees reached skeletal arms, yearning to embrace you forever; bark twisting into desperate, hungry faces, wild eyes wanting you to leave the warmth and join them in the cold Otherworld.

Twigs delicately stretch into fingers, those hands reaching out of the book, grasping, wrapping themselves around my neck, a breath, a growl, the Faun; Rackham's tentacles roiling wetly through time's labyrinth into Del Toro's brain, and mine, on some fifth-dimensional space shit. Centuries earlier, a Metaphysical poet wrote about the death of his faun, not knowing Rackham would supply the raw materials for Del Toro to bring it back.

Monsters sketched out of the thinnest air, taking sometimes gentle form, sometimes brutal. The dream decides. The dream leads the dreamer, here by the hand, there by grabbing a fistful of hair and drinking up my screams as it drags me into its maw.

As Rackham's ghostly forms evolved in my echoing self, those roots burrowing and tentacles rising, they made space for more. Werewolf children haunted the '70s *Hammer House Of Horror* while hammers of fascistic terror marched past kids being fed into a meat grinder only to be turned into fleshy worms that crawled through my soul forever after.

All just "Another Brick In The Wall" of horror, the hammers were followed by vengeful spirits animating clowns and trees, with more branches turning into claws as the Poltergeist took over the suburban home. Rackham's trees still reached through time, curling around the edges of space, pulling back reality to reveal the Otherworld, allowing an endless procession of ghosts to march through my bedroom all night after watching the movie.

They're here, at least in the nightmare. Assuming that it was a nightmare.

Traumatic hallucinations, perhaps. The tangled, moving, fully alive roots of horror in my soul, *The Beast From 20,000 Fathoms* screaming within the skeletal roller coaster as black-and-white fire engulfed it, a mind poisoned by alcohol sent desperately into darkness—Ray Bradbury's original beast lured by The Fog Horn, all alone and crying out, cries that will never be heard, lost in an all-encompassing emotional void; a never-ending darkness so complete that imaginary horrors are the only companions, gibbering and hollering and hissing.

In the real world via '80s paperback covers, tears of blood fall from lonely eyes. A man grapples with a giant wasp. Pale crosses that loom from the shadows try in vain to exorcise demons who will never stop, the hammers of fascism still stalking the world while children are fed into the meat grinder, over and over again. That army of poltergeists shackled by a greater evil still marching with ceaseless shuffling in a procession overseen by a devil that could, according to one of the scary stories we made up in kindergarten, knock the world off its axis, out of its orbit tumbling into space, while every human drifts helplessly away into asphyxiating infinity.

As writers, creatives, we hide from that infinity as much as we seek it, curling up for comfort in the roots of Rackham's tree, nourishing the flourishing of horror as decades and centuries pass. We let the roots slither around us, hold us ever so tightly, maybe too tightly, maybe over time they infiltrate us as we disappear into them.

And still the tree continues to grow.

Always hungry.

Told in the Dark

by P.N. Harrison

Colorless, a cheek is torn by arachnid limbs. Ink-drawn, a head rolls from a fireplace to a boy's feet. Images pressed into malleable minds. Peers passed the pages, sharing the shock of the sketches.

But my interests dwelled at the books' backs. Printed there was the research, the facts that inspired the images. The folklore of fear for the curious minds. Though the drawings frightened me away, the legends sang a siren's song that called me back. In time fear faded, but my curiosity continued.

Decades later, film homages the illustrations, but not their history. But I am curious still.

CREEPSHOW

ESSAY BY REX BURROWS

No, not the movie.

In July of 1982, the Plume imprint of Penguin Books published a comic book adaptation of *Creepshow*, a horror anthology film slated for release later that fall. It would feature five segments written by horror icon Stephen King and directed by the similarly legendary George Romero. The comic version swapped out Romero's camera for the pen of artist Bernie Wrightson, a horror luminary in his own right whose credits included co-creation of the DC Comics character Swamp Thing as well as contributions to the horror magazines *Creepy* and *Eerie*. The cherry on top was the cover from *Tales from the Crypt* and *Vault of Horror* artist Jack Kamen, a direct link to the pulp horror comics of the 1950s that serve as Creepshow's primary inspiration.

Obviously, I didn't know any of that when I first encountered the book at the age of eight.

I didn't know who Romero, Wrightson, or Kamen were, and my only knowledge of Stephen King was as a name on the covers of some intriguing books that I wasn't allowed to check out of the library. I was just an unsupervised third grader trying to be inconspicuous while creeping among the shelves of a bookstore in Bozeman, Montana's lone mall. My mother had left me to wait in the store by myself while she attended to other shopping (yes, I'm aware this is not even remotely up to spec by current parenting standards). My family had only recently arrived in Bozeman after our fourth cross country move, and it would be less than a year before our next relocation. I'd settled into my status as the perpetual new kid at whatever school I happened to be enrolled in. Immersing myself in books, comics, and movies helped pass the time while I tried to make a new set of soon-to-be-left-behind friends.

My rootless upbringing (among other things) contributed to the development of an anxious kid prone to jumping at shadows. Counterintuitively, my relationship to the creepy end of pop culture was that of an iron filing drawn to a powerful magnet. Lurid movie posters and video boxes, action figures modeled on monsters, Saturday afternoon creature features on local UHF channels—these were the kinds of things that attracted my immediate and focused attention. As horror writer Nadia Bulkin and others have noted, it's not unusual for children struggling with stress or anxiety to gravitate toward small, manageable doses of fright that can serve as inoculations against more serious worries and fears. Horror in this context can be calming and even therapeutic; it certainly was for me.

This is all to say that on that afternoon in 1982 in a run-of-the-mill, fluorescently lit mall bookstore, Kamen's cover for *Creepshow* seemed to literally leap out at me. The title is rendered in a spiky, dripping font that instantly signals "Horrors Found Here." Below it, a young boy sits in his bedroom clutching a comic book, one that itself bears the title *Creepshow*. The walls are plastered with horror movie posters: *Dawn of the Dead*, *Carrie*, and *The Shining*. And behind him, just outside the window, hovers a cloaked and skeletal figure with its single staring eye fixed not on the boy on the bed but rather YOU, the unwary reader of the book. For me, this imagery translated to one clear message:

This is something special. This is something for you.

As for the interior subject matter, it's difficult to describe the specifics of Wrightson's gory, lovingly rendered panels while avoiding overt spoilers. Creepshow's *Tales from the Crypt*-style twist endings and the delivery of horrifying comeuppances to the wicked are half the fun though, so I'll try not ruin anything for the uninitiated. I'll just say that the dead rise from their graves in distinctly worse for wear condition, hungry things emerge from antique shipping crates, and severed heads are put to creative new uses. This wasn't the gently spooky material I was accustomed to, the Universal monster movies with their misty cemeteries and drafty, cobwebbed castles. This was the real thing—this was *really* scary.

I sat cross-legged in a corner of the store flipping through the pages, entranced and not quite believing what I was seeing. Compared to the more transgressive frights that would arrive a few years down the line with the splatterpunks, *Creepshow's* scares are fairly tame, charmingly retro even by the standards of the 1980s. For me though, at that particular moment, it was dazzling stuff, utterly terrifying in the best possible way. Were people even allowed to write things like this, much less draw them? I knew I'd strayed well beyond the bounds of age-appropriate reading material, but nothing in the world was going to pry that book out of my greedy, grasping hands.

Until, of course, something did.

"Come on, it's time to go."

Engrossed in my reading, I'd failed to notice my mother returning to the bookstore to collect me. I snapped the book closed and quickly scanned the cover image with a more critical eye. It was creepy but not outright horrific, and I'd accumulated just enough allowance money from chores and good grades to afford the price. So long as my mother didn't inspect the interior pages, the book might slip under the radar of parental approval and accompany me home. I got up off the floor and presented the book.

"Can I get this?"

I'm sure I looked as casual as an eight-year-old can when he's trying to get away with something, by which I mean not very. My mother took the book, gave the leering ghoul on the cover a quick glance, and reached a swift (and probably sensible) verdict:

"No. Put it back. It'll give you nightmares."

The judgment was rendered and further arguing was pointless. I sulked back to the rack where I'd found the book, disappointed but taking consolation in the fact that I'd already attained some small measure of victory. The nightmares were on their way.

Enter the Void: Exploring the Cosmos and Beyond

Endless night, primordial depths, eldritch terrors, and unimaginable monsters. The coupling of science fiction and horror centers our fears of the unknown and the existential dread that comes with it. Here, you will find encounters with that which make us feel infinitesimal, the ramifications of our humanity, and the lifelines that ground us in the vast expanse of the universe.

Whispers of the Primordial Deep

by J.D. Harlock

Blasphemous melodies of eldritch lore
are whispered to me in the eerie night.
And yet, enraptured by their cryptic core,
a throe grips me within its dark delight.

For a path from Innsmouth shall be revealed,
once this cruel conversion is complete.
And Mother promises me a life congealed,
as I meld with *His* ethereal fleet.

Till then, in the hush of the witching hour,
I lend an ear to our ancestral chime.
Its chant of indescribable power
shares their secret in primordial rhyme:

Bound to the abyss under Father's eye
Inside Y'ha-nthlei, we will never die ...

Purposeful Grimaces and Terrible Sounds

Essay by Vaughn A. Jackson

If you know me, you know I can give dissertations on dissertations about Kaiju. Sadly, I only have a brief segment here to captivate you with my knowledge, so I'll try to keep this short and focused. My first Godzilla movie that I remember—and thus my first Kaiju film—was *Destroy All Monsters (1968)*, the one where the aliens brainwash all the monsters to wreak havoc around the world.

Or the *first* of the Godzilla movies with this premise, I believe.

Because of this, I was introduced to several monsters all at once: the more popular ones like King Ghidorah, Mothra, and Anguirus, and the lesser known ones, like Manda, Gorosaurus, and Baragon. And of course, Godzilla.

Now, from about 1964 to 1975, Godzilla left his horror roots behind and slowly became more of a kid-friendly, hero of justice character, fighting off evil monsters who want to encroach on his territory—er, harm the human world—with stylized wrestling moves. On one occasion Godzilla even celebrates his victory with an iconic jumping dance.

This campy revitalization of a classic monster is what I grew up with, and it wasn't until much later on that I saw *Godzilla, King of the Monsters (1956)* and even later that I finally saw *Gojira (1954)*. Regardless, this started in me a great love (read: obsession) with giant monsters, and creature feature type movies in general. *Ultraman (1966)* was a close second in my heart, with my favorite monster being the Baltans, because of their laugh.

Like evil Santa Claus.

Gamera (1965), Colossal (2016), Cloverfield (2008), Pacific Rim (2013), to this day, I will watch just about any of them, no matter how bad. *Velocipastor,* I'm looking at you.

You don't get a date.

I *love* monsters. And I love a cool design, but here's the thing. The less of the creature I see, the better. At least from a horror standpoint. The original Godzilla has about 15 minutes of screen time in the approximately hour-and-a-half-long movie. Sixteen percent of *Gojira* is actually Godzilla. The rest is his wake, his aftermath, the destruction he causes, and the people he affects.

The rest, is the horror.

It lies not with the monster itself, but with the cataclysm that the monster brings. Sure, even in those campy older Godzilla movies, looking back, you can be pretty sure people are getting mushed and incinerated, but it's not shown, so you can still laugh when Godzilla does his little sumo dance, or chastises his—hideously ugly—son Minilla for not being able to use his Atomic Heat Ray properly. But when you focus on the people …

In *Gojira (1954)* the scene that always terrifies me the most is completely devoid of Godzilla, save in effect. A mother and daughter are in a house that is shaking and falling down around them as Godzilla, unseen, is destroying their home village/town. The mother brings her daughter close, and says, "Don't be afraid, we'll be where Daddy is soon."

Chills, *every single time.*

It's thirteen seconds of film and it is devastating. It's horror at its deepest and most emotional core. Because that's what horror is; it's raking claws against the emotions that make us uncomfortable. It's a stake through the heart of safety and normalcy. Horror and despair go as hand-in-hand as horror and hope, because you can't have one without the other. Hope and despair, that is. It was during a rewatch of this movie, after my first Kaiju novel was published, that I realized that what I wanted to write wasn't science fiction, it was actually horror. I wanted to elicit this emotion, this dark, heartbreaking empathy for people you don't even know.

Despair and hope, arms linked on the way to prom. Isn't that the essential state of mankind? Always trying to hold on to the best, even during the worst. Horror is human.

So while Godzilla is what got me into *creatures, Gojira* got me into horror.

But not because of the monster.

To reiterate, this is a scene completely devoid of Godzilla on screen.

Another example of this scenario is *Jaws (1975)*. The movie *terrified* people so much they didn't want to go to the beach, but the shark is only in it for four minutes!

Alfred Hitchcock once said, "I prefer to suggest something and let the audience figure it out. The big difference between suspense and shock or surprise is that in order to get suspense, you provide the audience with a certain amount of information and leave the rest of it to their own imagination."

To bring this back to my point: Monsters are scary. What the monsters *do*, is horror.

This is my approach, and my desire for the genre. I don't want an endless litany of jump scares, I want my chest clenched so tight my heart can barely beat. I want to sweat through my hands and never know exactly what's coming. I want tension.

When will the shark appear? What does this horrifying monster that devastates cities simply by being in them look like? Who is, and how are they, being affected by its presence? Everything I write has a monster in it, but sometimes that monster doesn't appear until halfway in the story. Sometimes you never get the full picture of what it looks like. But you always see what it does.

Because what you don't know … can hurt you.

BENEATH CLOUD NINE

BY VAUGHN A. JACKSON

Coiled, smoky tendrils hung from the underside of the cloud as it drifted over the town of Quiet Lake like an inky black jellyfish tantalizing its prey. It arrived, eclipsing the vibrant summer sun and plunging the residents into a soul-dampening darkness. Marie leaned out her bedroom window and shined her flashlight up at the curling wisps. The weatherman swore up and down that today should be bright and warm enough for cookouts and all manner of outdoor activities. Each hour he'd appear back on their TV wearing his crisp blue suit and nervous smile claiming that the strange formation would roll away with the wind soon enough.

Still the cloud remained. It squatted over Quiet Lake like a grotesque toad on a lily pad. And Marie didn't feel any wind. The air was dead and heavy, as though the whole world were waiting for the encore to some unknown show. Marie shuddered as a crop of goose bumps broke out on her arms despite what remained of the noon heat.

The sound of heavy footsteps pulled her attention from the sky to the street below. She lived on the town's main thoroughfare, and often talked with people as they passed. She recognized the haggard, multilayered attire of Sean Navarro. Everyone knew Sean and treated him kindly—or as kindly as any relatively well-off person could without patronizing him—despite the plethora of odors and critters that lingered around the man like an aura. Marie once asked her father why no one just let the man live in a house. He had assured her that Sean enjoyed his homeless lifestyle; Marie wasn't convinced.

Sean waved up at her as the beam of her flashlight fell upon him. He flashed a nearly toothless smile and said, "Evening, young lady."

"You'd better take cover soon, Sean!" Marie glanced back up at the cloud covering. Something slithered within the rolling blackness. She rubbed her eyes, and looked harder.

Nothing moved.

"It"—she hesitated before looking back down at the homeless man—"looks like rain?"

He tilted his head back and laughed. "Well it won't be the first time I've been rained on."

"That doesn't sound good." Marie squinted, a thinking habit she picked up from observing her father when she asked one of her many questions. "Maybe you could stay with us until—"

The first drops of rain plummeted heavy and thick like pen ink, and just as black. Before Sean could respond, the levee in the sky broke and a torrent of black came crashing down like a waterfall. Marie recoiled, pulling away and narrowly avoiding getting soaked from on high. She slammed the window hard enough to shake the curtain rods above it.

The young girl and the homeless man shared a silent moment, one looking up through a curtain of black rain with a shroud of confusion shadowing his face, the other peering through a glass pane with a feeling of trepidation that grew like mold across her soul. Water oozed in thick streams—a network of corrupted veins—down the glass, and pooled on the external sill. Marie wanted to open her window again. She wanted to call out to Sean and tell him to get out of the rain, but the accumulating fluid—it grew harder for her to think of it as water—trembled like gelatin, refusing to tip over the sill and pour down to the ground.

It *clung*.

Fear spurred Marie's heart into a gallop as she realized that she could no longer see Sean. Not all of him, anyway. His silhouette—an odd negative against the otherwise black downpour—stood in the same spot, face angled toward the sky. The figure pulsed with a grayish light, as if the rain were highlighting him.

Marie pounded on the window, trying to get his attention, but the homeless man didn't seem to hear. If he did, he made no effort to acknowledge her. Marie banged harder, then stopped, her hand frozen against the cool glass of the pane. The rain around Sean's glowing silhouette shifted. Marie pictured something moving over his head and blocking the rain in a slow, sweeping motion.

Something that coiled and wound about, dangling like a worm at the end of a hook.

Marie remembered the flicker of movement in the clouds. She glanced up, but the torrent of dark water obscured everything overhead. Still she couldn't shake the feeling that some eldritch fisher stooped above them, tempting and tantalizing; an irresistibly delicious promise of a cruel fate.

Thunder cracked like a bullwhip, and a quick, sharp screech ripped its way from Marie's throat. She searched the ground for Sean once more, but he was gone. Her eyes darted around, scanning the darkness for any sign of his light. With each pass, the fear in her veins pounded hard until its drumbeat drowned out all other sounds. She hadn't realized she'd started to scream until her father, Dennis, burst into the room, driving out the darkness with the halogen yellow light of the hallway.

"Marie?" Dennis's eyes drooped with the exhaustion that comes from a sudden and unexpected awakening. His work kept him up late, and he often slept until well into the afternoon if Marie let him. He pushed long brown hair back from his face and scanned the room, looking for the source of his daughter's scream. "What's wrong? Did you have a night—" He paused, realizing that it was supposed to be noon. "Oh, was it the storm?"

"Yes! No! It's Sean. I was talking to him through the window and then the rain and the cloud, and then he … he's gone!"

Dennis frowned. "Gone? Like he left? You know he doesn't—"

"The sky ate him!" Marie turned her wide eyes back to the window. Once more she searched for the homeless man. Black shapes writhed in the darkness, visible only as they displaced the rain along their winding paths.

Her dad crossed the room and stood beside her, placing a hand on her head as he squinted out into the black downpour. "Hell of a storm. Shame that man is caught out there in it."

"Can't you see them?" She asked.

The tired man glanced down at her with a raised eyebrow. His beard had grown short and scratchy recently, a testament to the hectic state of his work schedule. "The raindrops?"

"No!" Marie stomped her foot in frustration. "The … there are so many of them."

Dennis rubbed his eyes, seeming to finally, fully wake up. "You said Sean was out in this mess?"

Marie nodded.

"You're worried about him, yeah?"

Marie nodded again.

"Shit. Alright, I'll go get him."

Marie's heart plummeted into the pit of her stomach. A sensation of creeping frost spread out from the empty space in her chest. She gripped her dad tight around his waist and squeezed her eyes shut.

Dennis ruffled her hair. "Okay, okay. You don't have to thank me. It's what any good person would do."

"But ..." Marie couldn't get the words out before Dennis vanished from her room. In a few moments, she heard the front door open and slam shut. She stood, rooted to the spot until she heard her dad's voice from outside, calling for Sean. His words—muffled and distorted by the black waterfall from the sky—drew her back to the window.

Dennis's silhouette appeared in the inky dark much the same as Sean's before. A faint, grayish wisp of a form shifting through the deluge while he called out for the vanished homeless man.

The filmy glob of congealing rain covered more of her window, wriggling as though it was alive. At this point, Marie wasn't convinced that it wasn't. Her father strode back and forth outside, looking for the missing homeless man.

Marie watched for the strange movements in the rain.

Dennis patrolled the torrent unmolested long enough that a sense of calm began to flow into Marie—until a flash of crimson lightning lit the world outside her window. In that instant—in the blood red of the storm's light—she saw it all. Hundreds of vines dangled down from the curdled cloud overhead. Each one was no thicker than a child's jump rope, but they twitched and snapped like a tangle of furious snakes.

Darkness crashed back into reality, and Marie was left with nothing but the overexposed memory of what she'd seen.

Dennis's silhouette froze and—like Sean before him—tilted its head to the sky. Marie screamed and pounded on the window with violent, reckless abandon. Cracks spiderwebbed across the glass, and thin trails of oozing rain crept in through the gaps like sticky fingers reaching out for her. She recoiled, tears in her eyes.

Thunder crashed.

Marie clamped her hands over her ears, but the sound still rumbled in her skull. She didn't need to look. The sky had eaten her dad, just like it ate Sean.

Still crying, she crept into the corner of her room and tucked her knees to her chest. Her head felt too heavy to hold up, so she rested it on her knees hoping she'd drift off and wake up to find that this had all been a terrible nightmare.

Sleep didn't come easy. It rained forever—like the story of Noah she'd read in Sunday School—drowning the world while she huddled away from the window and the ever reaching streams of inky rain that crept through the cracks like worms gnawing into her brain.

There wasn't any rhyme or reason for the thunder claps. She couldn't count to see if the storm was moving away, not that it mattered—she knew it wasn't, at least not until it was full. Red lightning scorched the world with the same infrequent abandon, turning her room into a blood-soaked nightmare for brief seconds at a time. The only sure thing Marie knew was that with each earthshaking boom, a person vanished. Sometimes she'd hear their voices first—calling out into the downpour searching for someone or something—but eventually they'd always fall silent, and from then it was a matter of time before the storm's fishing hooks snatched them up with sonic explosions as their cover.

Time lost meaning as the day stretched on. Or maybe days passed. Marie hunkered in the corner until the muscles in her legs and back screamed in agony—and eventually she did fall asleep. Her dreams were dark, and full of slithering things that hunted her from the shadows. No matter how she ran or hid, they always caught up and devoured her; a legion of monsters she couldn't see.

When she finally awoke with a shout, it was day again; actual day. Light streamed in through the cracked window, replacing the nightmares of the storm with a normalcy that Marie found almost as upsetting. She wondered if it had all actually been a nightmare. For the horrors of the night before to be so absent no more than a single sleep later seemed wrong.

But clearly, day had come.

It took her several long moments and a number of false starts for Marie to climb to her feet and slowly pad her way to the window. She crept like she did when sneaking downstairs for a snack after her dad went to sleep. The caution felt both misplaced and wholly necessary; her brain rationalizing it as "just in case" while simultaneously chastising her for being a scaredy cat.

The window swallowed her vision and her eyes quickly adjusted to the new brightness. Marie frowned, then twisted open in a silent scream.

Everything outside was completely dry, as if it had never rained at all. No signs or shutters were damaged—or even out of place—and every house's trees and lawns were as pristine as they had been the day before. The only sign of the previous day's terrors were the cracks in her window glass and—scattered about the street and sidewalks alike— scorch marks accompanied by dozens of empty shoes.

A Visit from the Depths

by Jen Mierisch

My feet trod land again, but my churning mind remained at sea. By moonlight, pacing, I found my path blocked by Etienne.

His hair dripped with seawater and stank of fish. My heart hammered. Impossible. The Atlantic swallowed him.

Though his sunken eyes looked past me, Etienne grinned. Had he forgiven my greenhorn's mistake, the oil leak I failed to fix, the explosion that hurled him overboard?

Hope washed my heart when he raised his thumb.

Only when I spun, saw the demon's maw, felt its briny tentacles around my neck, did I realize Etienne's signal was not for me.

DEATH BY ~~CLOWN~~ KLOWN

ESSAY BY L.P. HERNANDEZ

I witnessed my first murder at the age of seven. It was a period of transition for my family, a handful of months removed from my parents' divorce, and we had not found our new normal. Two sets of eyes became one. I understood the patterns. The routines. I have to trust in this knowledge of myself to account for the gap in my memory. Because I used this skill to watch a person die.

Wrapped in pink cotton candy.

Blood drained.

At the hands of killer ~~clowns~~ klowns.

Did my older brother sneak the empty plastic clamshell into Mom's basket at Blockbuster while she wasn't looking? Was this during a sacred HBO trial weekend? Here, my memory fails me. I remember how the room felt, the windows flashing blue as car headlights washed over them. I remember my dreams after, the twitch of the blinds when the air conditioning kicked on to battle the Texas heat.

Killer Klowns From Outer Space is the first horror movie I remember watching. I forget the how or who was in the room with me because I was hypnotized by the bright colors and what I thought was good acting. I was appalled by the violence, implied and shown, parading across the sub-27-inch screen.

The movie was both nightmare fodder and a gateway. It was like learning there is a new form of matter, new colors in our reality. Santa was real. Why not ~~clowns~~ klowns from outer space who zapped humans with cartoonish guns, imprisoning them in cotton candy cocoons? That color, the pink of the cocoons, stayed with me years after the finer details of the movie were lost. It became the whole movie for me.

I had so many questions. Were the people inside the cocoons alive? Were they aware? Did they stay there forever? That final question echoes through my published works dating back to my earliest writing. In "Madness" a man who committed suicide wakes up in a form of purgatory cursed with performing the task associated with his final thought in life, which was the infinite monkey theorem. This suggests a monkey, given infinite time and a typewriter, would eventually produce the entire works of Shakespeare. Our main character is escorted to a room with an endless ream of paper passing through a typewriter. He's told, "The complete works. Then you can move on."

I still feel gross thinking about that scenario. What if he did succeed in producing the entire works only to fat finger an extra *e* in The End? And it had to be perfect? What if this purgatory persisted outside of the universe as we understand it?

In "Offerings to an Old God" the God does not kill its victims but traps them within its strange, cosmic body. Forever. Until the end of all things. The prospect of being devoured is frightening, but it's the equivalent of a jump scare. The idea of being a forced hitchhiker in a timeless entity, unable to affect or interact with your environment, only to perceive it, is a primal, gut-twisting terror.

I worried about the people in the cocoons, but something else stood out. When Mike and Debbie enter the circus tent spaceship, there are already several cocoons. Either the town was not the klowns' first stop of the night, or they've been harvesting for some time. What if it was a long time? A really, really long time.

Killer Klowns is, objectively, a pretty bad movie. So bad it's good, more precisely. And it is entertaining, which is more than I can say for some objectively *good* movies. It expanded my color palette. In its crude, bumbling way, it steered me toward new questions. These questions I am still attempting to answer three decades later.

Automated

by L.P. Hernandez

The last memory of before was a sky full of stars, not one of them brighter than it should have been. Venus rested beside the moon like a dewdrop on the point of a sickle. Other planets I could not name slept in their infinite canopy. I have nothing but time, so I revisit this memory often, searching for something out of place, a star closer to me than it was a moment before. Maybe a hum so subtle I dismissed it as the tremor of far-off running water.

The memory ends, not with a gasp or blinding flash of light but with a wall of black stretching to the heavens. When I next open my eyes, there is light, tinted pink. I am disoriented in a just-off-the-rollercoaster way. My brain changes shape in my skull, as if massaged by invisible hands. I wonder if I am in the process of being reborn. It is warm, womblike here. But how would I know to think this as a fetus?

My right arm throbs with dull pain at the crook of the elbow. A deeper ache pulses in my belly and other, private places. Below my neck, my body is immobile. I am a marionette with the strings cut.

"Hello?"

I try to yell this, but what passes my lips is more of a moan. Wasn't I just looking at the stars? Maybe I tripped and stumbled into a ravine, breaking my neck. It would explain some things, but not the whole picture. It would explain the paralysis but not the pink, not the warmth. Wasn't it cold outside? When I looked up to the stars, did I see my breath rising?

"Hello!" I shout, or attempt to.

"What?" I say in response to a sound that might have been a voice. Impossible to know how near, but it sounds both close and far away. My senses have not returned fully, including hearing. It feels like there is cotton in my ears.

"What?!" I yell again.

He, and I'm almost certain it is a *he*, responds, but I come no closer to understanding. That won't come for days, as the soft edges of his words and the words of others begin to stiffen. Before that understanding, there is the cycle. It runs on a schedule, but with nothing to mark the time I cannot track it.

It begins with cold in my belly, as if the acid in my stomach has become puddles of ice cream. My torso swells. I can sense the skin stretching. I cry out in pain. The others do not. Eventually, I will join them in silence. The pain in my arm feels different and soon I am too tired to notice what else happens to my body.

***

Weeks have probably passed. The closest person to me is named Jeff, an incredibly difficult name to parse with the consonants being so subtle and muffled by the material separating us. He is my guide. Though his words make sense, the story they tell does not.

I was abducted. Based on the information available and the memories of some who regained consciousness during the process, we were transported onto an alien ship, immobilized and imprisoned within what some described as pink cocoons. Like cotton candy. The sensations correspond to processes. Feeding, waste removal, and blood drawing. Other processes occur during sleep, which I do most of the time. Jeff suggests some sleep is not natural and indicates maintenance beyond the routine.

Jeff: *All of us were abducted. Some folks claim to remember the ship, but there ain't much overlap in their description of it. Some say it is a colorful craft. Others say it was too bright to know anything for sure. Maybe it's both. Maybe it was colorful from a distance and too bright to see close up.*

Like you, we woke in our cocoons. Like you, took a while to make sense of what others were sayin'. We learned from folks who were abducted before us just as your doin' now.

Here's the thing, man, you can't read this story in one sittin'. Not that we don't have the time for it. Got more'n enough of that. It's for another reason. The most important reason.

Me: *What's that?*

Jeff: *You gotta keep your mind together. Got to.*

Me: *Why?*

Jeff: *There's no place to go. It's just you in there. Your mind falls apart and it has no place to go.*

He ended the conversation saying he needed a nap. There were others around. Other voices. Some were directed at me, but I could not understand them at that time.

Jeff: *Oh, before I drift off, we got a bet goin'.*

Me: *A bet?*

Jeff: *Yeah. Where you were picked up from and what year.*

Me: *Oh, it was Michigan. Outside of Tawas. I was doing some night fishing.*

Jeff: *And the year?*

Me: *2025.*

Jeff: *Michigan! 2025!*

He shouted the words, and they were echoed by a dozen diminishing voices.

Me: *What year were you picked up, Jeff?*

Jeff?

***

I assume months passed, and Jeff offered more chapters in the story, including information about himself. He was taken in 1978 while deer hunting near Bandera, Texas.

Me: *1978? How old were you? You sound my age.*

Jeff said nothing for a minute. I thought he fell asleep.

Jeff: *That's another chapter in the story, I'm afraid. You said you're thirty, right?*

Me: *Should be. Birthday isn't 'til August.*

Jeff: *I was thirty-two.*

Me: *Thirty-two? You'd be like eighty!*

Jeff: *Yep.*

Me: *But you sound ...*

Jeff: *Yeah. That's the next chapter. What's pumped into us keeps us young. Keeps us from agin' at least. They take our blood and then make us young. Don't know what part of the cycle. Don't think it's the cold stuff in our bellies. Probably happens when we sleep.*

I felt a twinge then, a seed planted. I peeked ahead in the story, glimpsed a passage my mind could not grasp but study peripherally.

Me: *There's others older than you?*

Jeff: *That's accurate.*

Me: *A lot older?*

Again, he answered with silence. Sometimes he did this in lieu of answering the question. Other times, he just thought about it a while.

Jeff: *How you holdin' up? I mean, I get none of this is good. You gotta family and all. They're worried about you for sure. But how's your mind feel?*

Me: *Angry. Sad. My little girl will think I just left her. Me and her mom weren't getting along too well. Now she's in charge of the story. She can make me a villain.*

Jeff: *Hold onto it. Hold onto the anger but keep an eye on it. The first thing you need to accept about your situation is you're not in control. Your anger can give you strength. But it can also ruin you.*

Me: *Jeff?*

Jeff: *Yeah?*

Me: *You didn't answer me. Are there people here a lot older than you?*

Jeff: *How do you feel about what I said? About acceptin' you're not in control?*

Me: *Makes sense. Don't like it, but it makes sense. I wasn't much of a fighter back home. Fighting isn't even an option here, so …*

Jeff: *Then, to answer the question, yes there are people older than me.*

Me: *How much?*

Jeff: *She's too far away for you to hear. I can hear her sometimes, but we mostly talk through Ivan. Fatima is her name. From Argentina. Speaks twelve languages. Can you believe that? I mean, we got the time for it, but it's just not a skill of mine. I can do okay with Spanish, but that's about it.*

Me: *Yeah?*

Jeff: *She's kind of the social butterfly of the group. Tries to organize things, games and such, with as many folk as possible. Tries to keep our minds sharp.*

I was losing track of my question.

Me: *Yeah?*

Jeff: *That's why she's so good with language.*

Me: *What year was she taken?*

Jeff: *1915. But that's not important.*

Me: *1915?!*

Jeff: *Stay with me. Yeah, that's a long time ago. But I want you to visualize what I'm sayin'. We're all trapped in these cocoons. Two hundred and twenty-nine of us including you.*

Me: *Okay?*

Jeff: *It's like, oh, what's it called the sediment! Like how the soil is like a calendar. You can know when a volcano erupted because of ash in the sediment. It's like us. The further down the line you go, the further back in time.*

My heart beat faster in anticipation of his next words.

Jeff: *Fatima says there are folks down the line who don't speak any known language. She's never been able to understand them. Can't even tell what the base of the language is. That gal speaks old Germanic and Mayan. Learned to speak it here, I mean. She can't understand a word. Hasn't been able to in a hundred years of tryin'. Could be they lost their minds. There's a fair number among us who have.*

Me: *Or?*

Jeff: *Those languages are gone. Left no trace in our world. Means the people are probably gone, too, or absorbed into other peoples. So, if they ain't crazy, they're ancient. Not like ancient Romans. Not like ancient Egyptians. Older than that. Much older.*

***

I kept to myself after that. For a while. The seed in my brain was a sprout, the roots needling through gray matter. There were people on the craft who were thousands, many thousands, of years old. Thousands of years immobile. Thousands of years with a belly swelling with cold.

That might be my future.

Jeff: *You ready for the next chapter?*

Me: *I don't know. That last one was tough.*

Jeff: *I hear you. Think I about shut down for a few weeks after I heard it. But it ain't all bad. There's a certain sort of freedom in knowing you don't have a choice. Once you have the story and know your place in it, well then, the healing can begin. It's a good story too! Closest thing to an adventure we got among us.*

Me: *An adventure? What do you mean?*

Jeff: *One of us got free.*

Me: *What?! I didn't think that was possible.*

Jeff: *Don't get too excited. It was a fluke. His cocoon detached and broke open. All the tubes connected to him came out. He was just layin' there for a time. Chen was his name.*

Me: *Was?*

Jeff: *I'll get there.*

Me: *When did it happen? Was it before your time?*

Jeff: *It was. It was after Fatima got here. After she learned Chinese. Don't ask me the flavor of it. I can't ever hold those words in my head. Mandolin? Does that sound right? Happened before I got here by a couple decades maybe. Look, this is the most important chapter in this story. Do you wanna hear it or not?*

Me: *Sorry.*

Jeff: *It's okay. Just need you to listen, to really digest what I'm tellin' you. Now, Chen was on the floor for hours. Eventually, his limbs start tinglin' and he's able to turn his head. That's how we know what it looks like. Hundreds of pink cocoons hangin'. A few hours later, he's able to crawl a bit. Folk are talkin' to him, askin' him what he sees. Others are beggin' to be cut down as well. Chen was a mostly quiet fella. From what I hear, not the best person for this to happen to.*

Me: *What did he do?*

Jeff: *Crawled 'til he reached a, I don't know, a console or somethin' and pulled himself up. He's tellin' everyone about what he sees still. It's a big room, but there's not a lot of structure to it. It's just the cocoons as far as the eye can see. Eventually, he makes his way to the front of the line, to the first cocoons. Now, we haven't much talked about* **who** *they are. Who abducted us.*

Me: *You said—*

Jeff: *That was on purpose. Now, Chen explored as far as he could, but he was losin' strength. He wasn't hooked up no more, so he wasn't getting' any food or water. Just as he was getting' his legs under him, his body started rebelling. Wasn't hooked up to whatever keeps us young either, so he started aging quick.*

Me: *Jeff, do you know what abducted us?*

Jeff: **What** *is the right word for it.*

Me: *What do you mean?*

Jeff: *What. Not who. What abducted us was a spaceship. Who abducted us …*

Me: *I don't—*

Jeff: *Doesn't exist.*

Me: *What? What does—*

Jeff: *The ship is on autopilot, friend. I think that's the right word for it. There's no one at the wheel. There's evidence they were around. Sleeping quarters, uniforms. Strange ones from what Chen said. There's weapons. Also strange. Too many colors. That's what Chen said. Mighta got lost in translation. Said there was a viewing area, a window. He could see the moon and the earth beyond it. The ship was just sitting there. Waiting. He took a downturn. He was starving and aging by the minute. Tried to climb back inside a cocoon, but it doesn't work that way. It's automated.*

Me: *So that means …*

Jeff: *Could mean a lot of things. Remember, you're not in control of any of it.*

Me: *But if it's automated, it could go on for …*

Jeff: *That's right.*

Me: *Forever.*

Jeff: *And you'll feel every minute of it.*

You're Traveling Through Another Dimension

Essay by Aleco Julius

If you read the title again, I bet you can hear these words. I am also willing to bet that you can hear the eerie music that accompanies them, which never fails to send a slight chill up your spine. You hear that unmistakable voice of narration. Perhaps you also think of spirals, clocks, and the vast blackness of space. These are the images that make up my earliest memories of the strange, the wonderful, the sometimes terrifying. And whenever I hear these words, I think of my dad.

Grief is an interesting thing. A phenomenon I knew existed because I had witnessed it in others. But observation is no substitute for direct experience. I have lost people close to me, and what happened is that the sorrow sort of mutated into memory. It congealed like tissue and became a part of who I am.

When I lost my dad, however, it was more like a bomb going off without warning. The resulting pain is a slow-motion ever-expanding shockwave. As time passes, the wave of pain may subtly weaken, but the circle continues to expand farther out, unavoidably encompassing every part of my world. His sudden death has forced me to continue with an altered point-of-view, a reorganized cognition. It is akin to a lens through which the permanence of things, of people, is fleeting. The present moment is imbued with heavier gravity, where the past lies just beyond the outer edge of the wave.

The strange, the wonderful, the sometimes terrifying. These are words that I often use to describe my own writing, and certainly the words that come to mind in the recesses of memory regarding my very first experiences with this macabre work—this art—that we all love.

It is a cold winter night, and my dad and I are up late watching *The Twilight Zone* marathon on TV. My two brothers are asleep upstairs in their room, and, being the eldest, I am allowed to stay up past my regular bedtime. Since it is New Year's Day, there's no school tomorrow. My mother is asleep, too, although the intoxicating scent of her cinnamon tea is still in the air of our little home. My father microwaves extra buttery popcorn, one of his favorite snacks, and pours the steaming bag into two bowls. The room is lit low by the single lamp on the corner table.

The chilling opening music emanates from the boxy TV set on our living room floor. *You are traveling through another dimension. Not only of sight and sound but of mind.* The narration continues until the brass crashes, and the camera pans down to a woman lying on a hospital bed, her head fully bandaged all around. I am immediately struck by the deep shadows, the angular contrasts of the interior architecture. Each character's voice is unsettling. I associate the tone of their words with worry and suffering, and it reminds me of the inside of a nightmare. As I watch, I notice my dad's sly smile. I realize later that he had previously seen this episode, and knew what was going to happen. He smiles because it is a fresh experience for me, a door opening into new sensations and emotions, even a new perspective.

He was right, of course——and this fascination, this attraction to strange and unsettling stories has stayed strong with me ever since. During the closing credits of the show, with the return of the eerie outro music, my dad asks me what I think of the episode titled, "Eye of the Beholder." I don't remember my response, except for the thrill and wonder coursing through my blood. It was an injection, like an infant's lifelong vaccine, eventually flowing into my writing. Stamped onto my consciousness and revealed in my work.

Recently I read a book by Anne Serling called *As I Knew Him: My Dad, Rod Serling.* In the afterword, she writes that one of her goals in writing the book was "to navigate that minefield of grief after my dad's death." Rod Serling, the creator and narrator of *The Twilight Zone,* was one of my dad's favorite figures, and consequently one of my top influences. Reading Anne's book after my own dad died provided a way to negotiate my own grief as I observed the parallels in our experiences. Rod and Anne were father and daughter, but also best friends. Rod was funny, silly, and generous in his love with everyone around him. Rod often talked about his youth, and valued memories and storytelling. Rod died unexpectedly of a heart-related affliction.

As Anne recalls certain episodes written by her dad, I stop reading and watch the episode. Each viewing transports me back to the tradition my dad and I shared of watching *The Twilight Zone* New Year's marathon. These stories taught me that there are multiple sides to the human condition, and that the most difficult experience is change. The greatest stories are truly about change. Shifts in perspective, developments into new understandings, the joy of birth and pain of loss. It is therapeutic to write about my dad and realize that my inaugural encounters with the strange, the weird, the sometimes terrifying were with him. It's like traveling through another dimension, whose only boundaries are that of imagination.

LAGNIAPPE

During a staff meeting one gloriously stormy night, the idea of having a section titled "Lagniappe" near the end of anthologies published by Brigids Gate Press was discussed. The staff unanimously voted in favor of the idea.

Lagniappe (pronounced LAN-yap) is an old New Orleans tradition where merchants give a little something extra along with every purchase. It's a way of expressing thanks and appreciation to customers.

The Lagniappe section might contain a short story, a poem, or a nonfiction piece. It might also feature a short novella. It may or may not be connected with the theme of the anthology.

The extra offering for this anthology is written by Scott J. Moses, whose essay "On Ending" and short story "If You Need Peace, Look No Further Than Beneath Your Floorboards" are a perfect summation of grief, loss, horror, and their connection to the human experience.

Enjoy!

ON ENDING

ESSAY BY SCOTT J. MOSES

*"but the special characteristic of a great person is to triumph over the disasters
and panics of human life." —Seneca, On Providence, 4.1*

To be born human is to enter this world as an empty vessel for loss. All
of us vacant for it. The word, *loss,* synonymous with the word, *human.*
Sides of the same coin.

Human beings.

Losing beings.

Consciousness, as far as recollection serves, began with one of two
memories. Me, a child in a blue jacket, the autumn in bloom, and sitting
in a pumpkin patch, and (or?) me waking to awareness as my dad holds
me off the side of a ferry, asking my mom if he can let me go. Both deal
with death, even if my child's mind didn't know it. The slow dying
change of summer into autumn. The concept of an end. Churning water
beckoning me somewhere new or nowhere at all.

My heart thumped, I remember that much, and that I was open-
mouthed and smiling, though I didn't know why.

I think this had a hand in why I took to horror. I've always had this natural
bend to melancholia and the grave, and horror is perhaps the only genre in
which we truly reflect on our core fears as human beings. Horror is a way to
look at all the inevitability of the world and still stand upright. A way to
explore everything we dread as if looking in a mirror, and though we glimpse
ourselves, we're more homed in on what's behind us without having to see it
full on. We know *what* it is, or do we? Maybe it isn't until later, years perhaps,
that we realize a story meant what it did to us. We're just enveloped in a good
yarn, even as our subconscious is soothed without our wherewithal.

Death. Loss. Grief. Fear. Terror. Time. Love. Life. A good horror story makes us mindful of these things.

"Store surplus, be stronger, stand out, provide, avoid exile from the pack, etc." These subconscious goals our primitive brains lay out for us in our everyday. Goals we sometimes don't even realize we're attempting to sate. But the brain's just doing its thing. See, its function is screaming about this all hours of each day to keep us safe and *alive*, but as Mark Freeman says, "The brain is far from our best organ." The mind, *that's* actually us. The brain is no more than a probability machine giving us bouts of indigestion. An idea man, and an annoying one at that.

Ever stood somewhere high with no intention of ending things, and your brain gives you the thought you could jump? It works like that in *many* ways. Pitching us useless ideas and leaving us to parse out what's beneficial and what's garbage. The 'we' who realize we have these thoughts, *that's* what sets humans apart from other animals, for better or worse.

But if those were my earliest memories, I must also mention my earliest remembered dreams. The first is of Jack Skellington slaughtering my entire family in a large multiplex tree house, moving closet to closet, where we all hid, and finishing us off one at a time. I didn't see the movie until my twenties, so the jury's out on where that one came from. The second is of me in a beautiful, green-sheened lake near a roaring waterfall, drowning. I remember telling my parents about that one in our small, worn kitchen in the woods of Virginia. I can't remember the looks on their faces, but I wish I could.

I think it all goes back to that ferry for me, looking at the whipping, frothing torrent beneath my floating form, and having just come into awareness, being throttled with the fact that said awareness might end. That things aren't necessarily permanent, that they cease, and that that's okay and, what makes life beautiful. And I think, for a time, it's normal to grieve this end, knowing it's coming. Hell, I was all but paralyzed by it for several months not all that long ago. But what is grief but unexpressed love? See, the more we grieve, the more we loved and love *still*. Mortality may be one of the only things we can use our grief-of-an-end over to create more love, level up while we're here, and to live more fully knowing we're racing to an end, or at least an end to what we currently know.

You're held and looking out over the rusted white railing of an immense ferry. The churning water nipping at your toes beneath your swinging white tennis shoes. Turning right, left, to everyone existing in this moment dangling there as well. Those held by chance, good fortune or both, all spasming. Some kicking their feet. Some smiling and pointing to one another, seemingly unaware of the waves beneath us. Some petrified by the very thing many others don't seem to notice, terrified and thrashing in the arms of time, and yet, powerless, unable to remove their gaze from the roaring waters. Hardly blinking, as if the water calls for them, won't let them go, won't allow their attention elsewhere, because what's the point? They, never ceasing to wonder where one goes when dropped by our unseen binds. When they fall beneath the void current, never to be seen from this vantage again. Wondering if the descended stare up at us through the green sun-kissed sheen of that pulsing maelstrom with envy, pity, or medley of the two.

A pumpkin patch now, the fiery orange in stark contrast to the brown, decayed husks, dirt, and vines. We, lifting crisp dead leaves in our soft child fingers in fields of brown, knowing then that things end, and in that being the point, that it's all about *now*.

To be born human is to enter this world as an empty vessel for loss, and be that as it may, we're vessels for other things as well. Joy. Fear. Grief. Love. Wonder. Awe. That haunting capacity to ponder what if, to revel in uncertainty for a spell, and at the roads not taken. At how little control we all have.

So that all that's left is to close our eyes and feel that cool ocean spray on our tingling cheeks. The warmth of that distant, life-giving sun turning our lid-shielded visage orange red. The salt tang and brine on the air filling our lungs … *a panic rises in our periphery* … and we open our eyes to the one whimpering beside us, held as we are, as they thrash in the grasp of inevitability. Holding them until it doesn't. Utterly fearful at both circumstance and what's to come.

A light effort is all it takes, less a kick and more a brush of our shoe's sole against a bare calf to draw them from their suspended, bristling-with-panic anatomy. Their eyes asking a question we know well, have often asked ourselves:

Have you ever felt this way?

Returning their dread-laden gaze with a smile, asking a question of our own:

Don't you feel the sun on your face?

The time holding us isn't death row, but more the loving arms of an unseen father holding us aloft, allowing us to fly for a time, and to perceive the world in a way we might not have otherwise, doomed instead to forever misconstrue the waves and their message. Their meaning in the now. To realize for all our thrashing, we're wasting this gift we've been thrust into, and to take their hand in ours for a time, speak atop the roar of the waves.

"*I know,*" we say. "*I understand, but tell me …*"

Their lips split into the inkling of a smile, their hand squeezing ours as the tears come.

That's what good horror is to me, nostalgic, or otherwise.

If You Need Peace, Look No Further Than Beneath Your Floorboards

by Scott J. Moses

This isn't a ghost story, despite how much you want it to be. And yet, you're here—but of course you are. The leaves take flight in a sudden burst of wind with your trek up the walkway, anxious to be gone from your path, loathing to touch or be touched by you.

You smile at those before the graves of their loved ones, and they offer sympathy in reply, because why else would someone be here? To apologize to the long gone. To speak with them as if they never left. Surely, not to beg their forgiveness; for them to make all the misfortune—the consequences of your actions—disappear, as if that's what you deserve.

You pull up your collar for the gust coming in. The leaves scampering off on the asphalt now, their chatter bolstering your already rampant paranoia. You barely made it here. Your hands white-knuckling the wheel the entire state-to-state journey. Your nonchalant subcompact drifting over the yellow lines on the few hours' drive from your home— where most of it happened, and assumedly, *still does*—praying to every deity you've ever heard of to help you.

But where were these entities when your victims cried out for them? When you allowed them the chance to pray that final time? Even going as far as to wait seconds for a response from the godheads of their faiths, because you've only ever been curious, right? Longing for something or someone over us all, to give us structure. I mean, in all probability, wasn't just *one* of your many victims faithful and deserving of rescue? You paused—I'll give you that—before giving into the notion that in this world of billions, we are each *so very alone*. And so you gazed each in the eye while wrenching your hands around their throats, *my throat*, so they wouldn't be alone for once in their lives, if even just at the end.

But no, like with us, with *me*, there's no answer to prayer. I mean, if I didn't receive a reply, then why would any god exempt you from exclusion? Despite you sending Heaven and Hell a haul of souls these last decades, doing what you do. Hunting, though patient, what some might consider evil, but I—*we*—know better.

See, you and I both know we're all just humans making choices, and isn't that much worse than grandiose labels like good and evil? We're unpredictable, chaos with limbs merely bound to the whims of our ever-changing emotions. Boundless.

You extend your hands to my headstone, as if for some semblance of comfort. As if those tendons, muscles, and ligaments weren't the same which ended my time on the earth. I can't help but smile when you recoil as if the stone has teeth, like it's *burned* you. The embodiment of those legends which seem to limp on into our modern day—hallowed ground you're no longer able to caress.

Oh, now what's *this*? You're on your knees, slumped there as the wind picks up again. The leaves on the limbs above whisper in unison at this change, this facade. See, they don't believe you. Neither do I. And while you've yet to be caught, you more than deserve everything that's coming to you.

They know it.

I know it.

You know it.

Do you ever wonder why it's me haunting you and not any of the others? There were eleven victims total, yes? And don't look so surprised that I know of your latest, I mean, I know what you know, remember? But who other than me knows you still kill? No one. You're a rat, hard to banish, unseen, though always heard, always returning for what tempted you to begin with.

You're begging through snot and tears now, confessing as if I've the power to absolve you of your sins. Like I'm not the one orchestrating this hell for you. You tell me of inexplicable things: How the monkshood, though not native to this part of the country, keeps appearing on your doorstep and banister each morning. Interesting that monkshood—*Aconitum napellus, wolf's bane*—would be her flower of choice. And despite the phenomenon, you save them all. Placing each in an open trash bag in the basement near that latest unfortunate soul, because now you *miss her*, despite wrapping your hands around her pale throat that night in a drunken stupor. As if money being tight and hating yourself were reasons to take life. As if someone else were responsible for your misfortunes.

Pathetic.

How the crows and jays murder themselves en masse against your storm door, morning coffee shattering on the linoleum at your feet. They sense your wrongness, thrusting their tiny frames at you and what you've done. What you continue to do.

And like a heroin addict chasing a high, you long for the almighty rush had upon that first kill: your wife. The exhilarating uncertainty, of not knowing then how to adequately dispose of a corpse, of not knowing if you'd be caught, basking in the thrill of sheer *possibility*. But now? You're as someone who *thinks* that they enjoy certain holidays over others, when in reality they only ever ruminate on those past. Those once celebrated in happier times, and how they, you, haven't actually celebrated them in such a long while.

Killing is becoming mundane for you. That's why you're at this tombstone, isn't it? Because, as B.B. King said, *"The thrill is gone."* Not because of the remorse one might feel after decades of committing grand atrocities.

See, *I know you*. You're selfish … weak … scared, like the rest of us, though you slip on a mask when you're murdering, breathing, thinking.

Do you remember what you said before murdering me? I do. You said: *the only reason most people don't kill each other is because it would complicate their lives. But complication* excites *me. It's the only thing that does anymore.*

Remember?

I like to think you do, and also choose to believe there isn't a god alive that can save you.

You mention her perfume. How it snakes through the vents of your home, your once-wife's scent of strawberries and cream clinging to the wood panels of your living hell, driving you mad. I've gotten to know her, actually, and while she's given me unique inspirations with which to plague you, she's rekindled something in me I'd thought lost—*belief*—because someone like her couldn't have been an accident. That her love for you existed in our reality is proof enough in a capacity for miracles.

And now for the reason you've come all this way. If only you could see it spill from your blubbering lips. A plea, a *bargain*—that if you let the bound lamb you've yet to slaughter go, despite what it would mean for you, that all this might somehow end. That I'll simply nod, pleased, and call that *that*. But that's not how this works. See, the murdered are still just so, and they're crying for blood, but even more they crave your *fear*, your *mind*. They want it all.

And though you can't see it, my unhinged jaw looming over you as you find the gall to place a hand on my stone again, I feel a sliver of sympathy for you. Your tears are genuine, humbling even. But if you need peace, something to cling to and know with absolute certainty, you needn't look further than beneath your floorboards, because there are plenty of things worse than death. There's still someone down there, no? Starving, beaten, and abused. Not offering up the euphoria you so desperately crave … as if that's her fault.

We read somewhere that some monsters, if not all, feel guilt at some point. That it eats away at them from where their souls used to be outward, bleeding into their everyday lives. I read that somewhere, or did I? You'll have to let me know.

And there you go, *begging* again. Have you been listening to a word I've been saying? You're here because you're caught not by the laws of man, but by something worse. Something inescapable: *yourself*.

Have you ever stopped to consider that this is *you*? Some semblance of guilt built stone-by-bloody-stone since first killing *her*? The love of your former life. That maybe the birds and the monkhood, those voices you hear like a coma at night, are in your head? Maybe you need help, medication, or therapy—not to right what you've done, or evade consequence—but to stop it happening again. Perhaps, when it comes down to it, every one of us has a threshold, a limit, if you will, and when you reached yours, you began to break, began to haunt *yourself*. Though we're not convinced pills and a comfortable couch could ever begin to remedy something like that.

How can we truly know anything? See, I have to believe you're as lost as I am, if I *am* at all. Perhaps you can't see me because I'm you, or … maybe you *always see*. That chill kiss on your throat as that young woman wails up through the floor of your bedroom. Know it's our hands reaching up from the earth, from inside what good—if such a term can be or ever was—used to reside in you before you or the world you blame stamped it out. Gripping your limbs, pulling you taut, each of us needing a piece for ourselves, owed that much.

Are we even here? In this dank, stereotypical cemetery? Oh look, how the old woman at the grave near us casts pity on you. You can't stand that, can you? You're thinking of ripping her in two as we speak. So, go ahead—why not? Because whether or not you do or don't pull her from herself under this newly risen sun, whether or not you let that girl in your basement go the moment you return home, what's done is done, and well … *I'm having too much fun.*

See, I'm that whisper of doubt. That room for error. What some call a conscience, and that's the *real haunt*, no? That you haven't been able to kill me entirely. Quiet me over the years? Sure. Stamp me out altogether? No, and you aren't sure why … and though I'm hushed at times, I'm still there, *here*, like gravity on your tethered corporeal form, slowly killing you all the same. One tortuous second at a time.

Are we having this conversation? Is this a dream? Somewhere I'm finally loud enough to get through to you? The old woman goes far enough to walk over and hug you, and you know what? You accept the embrace, hell, you *return* it, because you need the comfort of one who hasn't a clue of the blood on your hands. And as she withdraws from you, you pull her close again. Think of holding her there till her arthritic bones break from the sheerness of your will. Of how you don't want anyone to abandon you again, even if you send them off, your hands around their throat, you still expect them to return to you. That old biblical myth, *unconditional love*, doesn't exist in this world. You murder with hands, and hands alone. Primal, no? Some old and forgotten way of ending that which draws breath.

So, brush yourself off, wave, and smile to the old widow as she goes. Cheer up, you, because after everything, I'm offering a solution. Seeing as you came all this way.

As said before, I'm no ghost, not like you wish I was, because that'd be too easy now, wouldn't it? No, I'm the festering guilt you've neglected, and I'm here till you die, baby. So go on, do us and the world a favor when you get home. A bowl of monkhood should do the trick, and who knows? A little oil and vinegar? Could be the best meal you'll ever have.

About the Authors

Christi Nogle is the author of the Bram Stoker Award® winning and Shirley Jackson Award-nominated novel *Beulah* as well as the short story collections *The Best of Our Past, the Worst of Our Future, Promise*; and *One Eye Opened in That Other Place*. Her work has appeared in many publications such as *Apex Magazine, Strange Horizons,* and PseudoPod. She was co-editor with Willow Dawn Becker of the anthology *Mother: Tales of Love and Terror* and co-editor with Ai Jiang of *Wilted Pages: An Anthology of Dark Academia*. Follow Christi at http://christinogle.com and across social media @christinogle.

Richard Leis writes literary, horror, and speculative poems and stories that have been published in *The Deadlands, F&SF, Nightmare, Impossible Archetype,* the *Timberline Review,* and other publications, including anthologies from Crone Girls Press, House of Zolo, Weird Fiction Quarterly, and Wising Up Press. He works on an active Mars mission.

Catherine McCarthy is a Welsh working class writer who weaves dark tales on an ancient loom. Her longer works include *Immortelle, Mosaic, A Moonlit Path of Madness, The Wolf and the Favour, The House at the End of Lacelean Street* and her most recent novella, *Death of a Clown,* which published May '25 through Sobelo Books. Her short fiction can be found in various publications, including *Gamut Magazine, Dark Matter Magazine* and *Haven Spec Magazine*. Time away from the loom is spent hiking the Welsh coast path or huddled in an ancient graveyard reading Dylan Thomas or Poe. Find her @ https://cmccarthywriter.substack.com/ or https://x.com/serialsemantic

Basile Inspiratie was born and raised in Libya. They spent their childhood travelling around the world writing and learning about various folktales and legends with a particular interest in Arabian and Berber mythos. You can find them at @BasilInspiratie on x.com (formerly twitter)

Roberto Cofresí Hopgood is a Puerto Rican (Boricua/Caribbean/ Latine) writer and searcher who's lived in Texas, Colorado, Mexico and New York City. Among other life affirming adventures, he survived being adrift on a boat on the Gulf of California, being lost without water in Barrancas del Cobre, being robbed by a one-eyed man with a penknife in NYC and being yelled at by Werner Herzog in Texas. He is the author of *Bellows: Fables from the Musical Underground*, and more recently his stories (in English and Español) have appeared in *Uncharted, LatineLit, Smokelong Quarterly, The Write Launch, Enclave, Evento Horizonte, Drunk Monkeys, Claridad* and more as well as in multiple anthologies. He currently lives in Chapel Hill, NC. Visit his website at https://rocofresi. wixsite.com/rchopgood/en

C.L. Prater The Rosebud Reservation of South Dakota had no public library. Thus, C.L.'s summer reading came from the dusty shelves, boxes and barrels of her uncle's backroom and barn. One book, a volume of *Alfred Hitchcock Presents: Stories for Late at Night*, introduced her to the likes of Ray Bradbury, Roald Dahl, and Frank Belknap Long. A retired teacher, her work has appeared in literary magazines and anthologies. Of late, she's ventured into subjects with a spookier feel.

Ngô Bình Anh Khoa is a teacher of English in Ho Chi Minh City, Vietnam. In his free time, he enjoys reading fiction and writing speculative works, many of which have appeared in *Penumbric, Eternal Haunted Summer, Star*Line, Weirdbook, Spectral Realms*, and other venues and anthologies. In addition to speculative works, he enjoys writing haiku, some of which have previously won awards and achieved honorable mentions in international contests in the US, Japan, Canada, and elsewhere.

Kate Falvey's work has been published in many journals and anthologies; in a full-length collection, *The Language of Little Girls*, and in two chapbooks, *What the Sea Washes Up* and *Morning Constitutional in Sunhat and Bolero*. A four-time Pushcart Prize nominee and a Best of the Net nominee, she co-founded (with Monique Ferrell) and for ten years edited the *2 Bridges Review*, published through City Tech (City University of New York) where she teaches, and is an associate editor for the *Bellevue Literary Review*.

Robert P. Ottone is the two-time Bram Stoker Award-winning author of *The Triangle* and *There's Something Sinister In Center Field*. He is also the best-selling author of *Curse of The Cob Man, The Sleepy Hollow Gang, The Vile Thing We Created* and *Nocturnal Creatures*. His short fiction has been collected in *Tear Me Open: Fears Unwrapped* as well as *Her Infernal Name & Other Nightmares*. He holds two master's degrees in Education, as well as an MFA in Children's Literature. A bagel-loving fabulist of spooky absurdity, Ottone enjoys cigars, cocktails and time with his wife.

Mir Rainbird is composed primarily of words. Mir's other interests include arguing with cats and being mediocre at art. For more words, read *Cosmic Horror Monthly, Trollbreath, Inner Worlds,* and various anthologies. For good cats and bad art follow @mir_rainy on Instagram. https://linktr.ee/rainbirdm

Ivana Geček is a Croatian writer and comic artist. She writes horror and weird fiction, often through a queer lens. Her short stories were published in various anthologies, as well as the Croatian speculative fiction magazine *Morina Kutija*. Her debut sapphic horror novella *Bye-Bye, Babaroga* was published in 2024 by Shtriga Books. In her spare time she likes to read about cryptids, pick at the banjo, and watch good and bad horror movies.

Xochilt Avila (they/them) is an indie horror author based on the US Eastern Coast. Their work has been published by Ghoulish Tales, Cursed Morsels, Tenebrous Press, and more. When not writing they can be found smooching their cats and planning their next meal. They are active on BluSky @xavilawrites.bsky.social, and you can find their publications at https://xochiltavila.carrd.co/

Jenny Lewis is a writer of dark and unsettling fiction, her stories often feminist driven, highlighting the "good for her" trope. Her upmarket suspense *Take Me Apart* is on submission and she's working on edits for a Southern Gothic Horror. She is represented by Claire Cavanaugh @The Rights Factory. Her work has appeared in *Erato Magazine, KCB the Mag, Women on Writing, Punk Noir Magazine,* and *Pretty Girls Make Graves: A Feminine Rage Horror Anthology*. Follow her @WriteJennyWrite on

Instagram, Threads, and BlueSky or check out her website at JennyLewiswrites.com.

Candace Nola is a multiple award-winning author, editor, and publisher. She writes poetry, horror, dark fantasy, and extreme horror content. She is the creator of Uncomfortably Dark Horror, which focuses primarily on promoting indie horror authors and small presses with weekly book reviews, interviews, and special features. Uncomfortably Dark Horror stands behind its mission to "bring you the best in horror, one uncomfortably dark page at a time." Follow her on all social media and join the Uncomfortably Dark Patreon for free books, merch, and more!

Angela Sylvaine is a Bram Stoker Award nominated author and self-proclaimed cheerful goth. Her novel, *Frost Bite*, a '90s sci-fi horror comedy, and her retro '80s YA mall slasher novella, *Chopping Spree*, embody her cheerful side. Her short story collection, *The Dead Spot: Stories of Lost Girls* is fully goth and heartbreaking. Angela's short fiction and poetry have appeared in over sixty anthologies, magazines, and podcasts, including *Southwest Review, Apex,* and The NoSleep Podcast. She lives in the shadow of the Rocky Mountains with her sweetheart and creepy cats. You can find her online at angelasylvaine.com.

Nick Mehalick is a queer poet who likes unpleasant truths. He is a son of Langhorne, Pennsylvania and author of the chapbook, *Melissa Etheridge's Seminal 1993 Album Made of Two Overlapping Triangles Instead of One* (2021), Ethel Zine & Press, has poems featured in *Big Backpack Full of Soup Cans: Malcontent Poems* anthology (March 2025), Alien Buddha Press, fiction in *Poisoned Soup for the Macabre, Depraved and Insane* anthology (December 2025) Brigid's Gate Press, and work in other fine literary journals and magazines. He teaches in Philadelphia, is the host of the podcast Book.Record.Beer. and drummer for various Philadelphia-based bands. Instagram: @iamdrums

Avra Margariti is a queer author, Greek sea monster, and Rhysling-nominated poet with a fondness for the dark and the darling. Avra's work haunts publications such as *Strange Horizons, The Deadlands, F&SF,* Podcastle, *Asimov's, Vastarien, Three-Lobed Burning Eye,* and *Weird Horror.* You can find Avra on twitter (@avramargariti).

Die Booth is an indie author who likes wild beaches and exploring dark places. When not writing, he DJs alongside his boyfriend at Last Rites—the best (and only) goth club in Chester, UK. You can read his prize-winning stories in anthologies from Egaeus Press, Neon Hemlock, Flame Tree Publishing and many others. His books, including his cursed novella *Cool S* are available online, and he's currently working on a queer coming-of-age folk horror novella. You can find out more about Die's writing at http://diebooth.wordpress.com/ or say hi on Instagram @dieboothwrites or Bluesky @diebooth.bsky.social

Amanda Hard writes poetry and short fiction from her home in the cornfields of Indiana. She earned her MFA in creative writing from Murray State University and her work has appeared in publications such as *Flash Point Science Fiction*, *MetaStellar*, and multiple anthologies and poetry collections. Find her on BlueSky: @catouttawater.bsky.social.

Michael Bailey is a recipient and ten-time nominee of the Bram Stoker Award, a five-time Shirley Jackson Award nominee, and a three-time recipient of the Benjamin Franklin Award, along with several independent publishing accolades. He has written, edited, and published many books. His latest is *Silent Nightmares*, an anthology co-edited with Chuck Palahniuk to be published in the fall of 2026. He is also the screenwriter for *Madness and Writers*, a creative documentary series about writers, and a producer for numerous film projects. Find him online at nettirw.com. He is represented by Lane Heymont of the Tobias Literary Agency.

Pedro Iniguez is a Mexican-American Bram Stoker Award-winning science-fiction and horror writer from Los Angeles. He is the author of *Mexicans on the Moon: Speculative Poetry from a Possible Future*, *Fever Dreams of a Parasite*, *Echoes and Embers: Speculative Stories*, and his debut picture book, *The Fib*, among others. Apart from leading writing workshops and speaking at several colleges, he has also been a sensitivity reader and has ghostwritten for award-winning apps and online clients.

Brian McAuley is the USA Today Bestselling Author of *Breathe In, Bleed Out*. His debut novel *Curse of the Reaper* was named one of the Best Horror Books of 2022 by *Esquire*. He also penned the holiday horror novella duology *Candy Cain Kills* and *Candy Cain Kills Again: The Second Slaying*. As a WGA screenwriter, Brian has written everything from family sitcoms (*Fuller House*) to horror films (*Dismissed*). He teaches as a Clinical Assistant Professor of Screenwriting at ASU's Sidney Poitier New American Film School. Connect with him on social media @BrianMcWriter

Tiffany Morris is an L'nu'skw (Mi'kmaw) writer from Nova Scotia. She is the author of the *Ignyte, Indigenous Voices*, Shirley Jackson, and Aurora award-nominated *Green Fuse Burning* (Stelliform Press, 2023) and the Elgin Award-winning horror poetry collection *Elegies of Rotting Stars* (Nictitating Books, 2022). Her work has appeared in the indigenous horror anthology *Never Whistle At Night*, as well as in *Nightmare Magazine, Uncanny Magazine*, and *Apex Magazine*, among others.

Diane Funston has always had branches for bones and leaves for hair. A true Daphne at heart, she writes poetry and memoir along with visual art in media of collage, mosaics, and wool felting. Diane appreciates, as a hometown New Yorker, her home in California where gardening is an everyday adventure and possibility. Previous publications include *F(r)iction, Lake Affect, Still Points Quarterly, Quiet Rooms, Woods Reader*, among many others.

Emily Ruth Verona is the author of Midnight on Beacon Street. Her ghostly novella, *Shiva*, is due out from Dark Matter Ink in 2026. She received her Bachelor of Arts in Creative Writing and Cinema Studies from the State University of New York at Purchase. She is a Pinch Literary Award winner, a Bram Stoker Awards® nominee, and a Rhysling Award Finalist. Her work has been featured in magazines and anthologies that include *This Way Lies Madness, Under Her Skin, The Ghastling, The Jewish Book of Horror, Under Her Eye, Monstrous Futures, Monster Lairs, Strange Horizons*, and *Nightmare Magazine*. She lives in New Jersey with a very small dog.

L. Stephenson has had a decades long career in media and the arts; reviewing movies for websites, working at concerts, interviewing bands, writing for radio, starring in short films, and copyediting for publishers. And somewhere in the middle of all that he even graduated university with a very useful degree in Film & TV Screenwriting … But what he loves doing, even more than his next cheeseburger, is being an author of horror stories. His first novella, *The Goners* blessed the world through CAAB Publishing in 2021 before expanding into his debut novel, *The*

Boatmore Butcher, published by Dark Ink Books in 2023. During this time his works also appeared in the Bram Stoker-nominated *American Cannibal*. His stories have haunted a number of anthologies, including *Unburied* and this year's *We'll Always Be Here*, which both benefitted LGBTQ+ charities. In 2024 he curated and edited the Christmas horror-themed *Violent Advents*, of which all royalties were donated to the American Heart Association and the British Heart Foundation. The following year, he independently released his first full-length collection *When Strange Things Bite* and was most recently signed to Truborn Press to release his second novella, *The Boy at No. 9 Whitlock*, which is due for release in August 2026.

Jan Stinchcomb is the author of *Verushka* (JournalStone), *The Blood Trail* (Red Bird Chapbooks) and *Find the Girl* (Main Street Rag). Her stories have appeared in *Bourbon Penn, Maudlin House* and *Gamut Magazine*, among other places. A Pushcart nominee, she is featured in *Best Microfiction 2020* and *The Best Small Fictions 2018 & 2021*. She lives in California. Find her at janstinchcomb.com; Bluesky: @janstinchcomb; Instagram: @jan_stinchcomb

Jillian Bost has been a fan of horror movies ever since she watched *Nightmare on Elm Street: The Dream Master* safely behind the couch. She has had several short horror stories published online and in anthologies, and is a member of the Horror Writers Association.

Erin Jo Eldry is a central Florida author, dabbling in both poetry and adult fiction. Selections of her work have appeared in various literary anthologies from Wild Ink Publishing and *Bunker Squirrel Magazine*. Eldry's debut novel, *A River Like Mine*, is slated for release in July 2026.

R. J. Joseph is an award winning, Shirley Jackson and Stoker Award™ nominated Texas based writer/professor/speaker. Her creative and academic work examines the intersections of race, gender, and class in the horror genre and popular culture. Rhonda is an instructor at The Speculative Fiction Academy and a co-host of the Genre Blackademic podcast. She has most recently been at work with Raw Dog Screaming Press on their new novella line, Selected Papers from the Consortium for the Study of Anomalous Phenomena. She occasionally peeks out on social media from behind @rjacksonjoseph or at www.rhondajacksonjoseph.com.

Darren Croucher emerges from the haunted, twisted depths of Bucks County, PA, to unleash horrors unimaginable (onto the page, to be clear). He has fully transformed from weenie to eldritch wielder of words, and is now ready to fulfill the literary promise of the first poem he ever had published, in high school, entitled "Death, Despair, Darkness."

P.N. Harrison is a writer of horror, weird fiction, and dark fantasy based out of the plains of Western Kansas. His short fiction appears in such venues as *Starlite Pulp Review* and the Graveside Press anthology *What Lurks: A Cryptid Anthology*. His debut novelette, *The Consort*, was recently released by Baynam Books Press. In his day job as an English professor, he has also penned numerous academic articles on topics such as H.P. Lovecraft, J.R.R. Tolkien, and books bound in human skin. When not muttering in dead languages, he enjoys watching baseball, travelling, and going on historic ghost walks with his wife, Ashley. He can be found online on Threads as pnharrison86, Bluesky as pnharrison.bsky.social, and at harrisonhorror.wordpress.com.

Rex Burrows writes speculative fiction, usually of the weird, dark, and unpleasant variety. His stories have appeared in publications including *Cosmic Horror Monthly*, *Weird Horror Magazine*, *Supernatural Tales*, and the *Horror Library* anthology series. He can be found on various social media platforms as @improbablerex or at www.rexburrows.com.

J.D. Harlock is an Eisner Award-nominated American writer, researcher, editor, and academic pursuing a doctoral degree at the University of St. Andrews, whose writing has been featured in *Strange Horizons, Nightmare Magazine, The Griffith Review, Queen's Quarterly*, and New York University's Library of Arabic Literature.

Vaughn A. Jackson is an author, editor, and sometimes poet of dark speculative fiction. His work generally falls into one of categories: Creatures, Kaiju, or Cosmic Horror. This often blends elements of fantasy, science fiction, and horror into one unholy abomination. His published novels include the Kaiju thriller *Up from the Deep,* and the cosmic horror novel *Touched by Shadows.* Vaughn is also the co-editor of *Beyond the Bounds of Infinity.* Vaughn is an Affiliate Member of the HWA, and secretary of its Maryland Chapter. He often cracks jokes and lives to make Lovecraft turn in his grave.

Jen Mierisch's dream job is to write Twilight Zone episodes, but until then, she's a website administrator by day and a writer of odd stories by night. Jen's short stories can be found in *parABnormal Magazine*, *The Arcanist*, NoSleep Podcast, Scare Street, and in numerous print anthologies. Jen can be found haunting her local library near Chicago, USA, where she lives with her husband, three pets, and two awesome Gen Z kids. She is currently working on a gothic horror novel set on a remote island. To read more, visit jenmierisch.com or connect on social media (@JenMierisch on BlueSky, Threads, and Instagram).

L.P. Hernandez is an author of horror and speculative fiction. His stories have been featured in anthologies from Dark Matter Ink and the Howl Society among others. He is a regular contributor to The NoSleep Podcast and has released three short story collections, including the recently published *No Gods, Only Chaos*. His novellas include *Stargazers* and *In the Valley of the Headless Men*. L.P. also hosts Dog-eared Nightmares, a podcast about well-loved horror. In 2024, L.P. partnered with fellow military veteran, L.C. Marino, to launch Sobelo Books, an indie horror press. He is a husband, father, and a dedicated metalhead. Instagram: authorlphernandez, sobelobooks, Threads: authorlphernandez, sobelobooks X: TheLPHernandez, sobelobooks Website: lphernandez.com, sobelobooks.com Tik Tok: authorlphernandez

Aleco Julius is the author of *Weird Tales of the Great Lakes and Endless Depths: Cosmic Themes, Weird Lore, & Hidden Knowledge*. His stories have appeared in *Dark Matter Magazine*, *Dolls in the Attic*, *Always Night*, *Writers Retreat*, *Anterior Skies*, *Red Line*, and more. His essays have been published by *Hellebore*, *Vastarien*, *Myth & Lore*, *Cold Signal Magazine*, and books by Anathema Publishing. He lives beneath the busy skies of Midway Airport in Chicago.

Scott J. Moses is the author of *Our Own Unique Affliction* (Shortwave Books). An Active member of the Horror Writers Association, his work has appeared in *Cosmic Horror Monthly*, The NoSleep Podcast, Planet Scumm, and elsewhere. He also edited *What One Wouldn't Do: An Anthology on the Lengths One Might Go To*. He is Japanese American and lives in Maryland. You can find him @scottj_moses or at www.scottjmoses.com. He is represented by Alec Frankel at IAG for TV/Film.

About the Editors

Wendy Dalrymple loves to explore the beauty in horrific things. She is a Florida-based author of feminist #pinkhorror, gothic and romance novels and has had her work published by a number of small presses as well as independently. She is the author of *Birthday Party Demon*, a nostalgic YA novella, as well as *Credenza*, a Florida gothic novel. Her upcoming pink horror novel *Bed Rot Baby* explores themes of self-image and body horror through the lens of the early 21st century, and her upcoming slasher novel *Killer Summer* is a nostalgic ode to her favorite teen horror films.

Grace R. Reynolds is an American speculative fiction writer. She was raised in New Jersey and graduated from Rutgers University. Having lived in seven states, she currently calls Maryland 'home,' where she writes dark fiction and poetry. In addition to her short fiction, she is the author of *Lady of the House* and two other collections of poetry. These include *The Lies We Weave*, which was nominated for the SFPA Elgin Awards, and *Midnight Blue*. Her debut novella, *Neon Moon*, will appear in the Spring of 2026 through Dark Matter Ink. Grace is an active member of the Horror Writers Association and the Science Fiction and Fantasy Poetry Association.

ABOUT THE ILLUSTRATOR

Alison Flannery is a slightly feral artist who lives and works in Denver, Colorado. Her work is inspired by nature and she works primarily in oil paint and paper collage, sometimes both at the same time. Alison's work can be seen on her website: www.AlisonFlannery.com

CONTENT WARNINGS

Abuse (child and domestic)

Alcoholism

Death

Grief trauma

Self-harm

Queerphobia

Racism

Xenophobia

MORE FROM BRIGIDS GATE PRESS

Blood in the Soil, Terror on the Wind

ed. Kenneth W. Cain

Whether in an old weathered mine shaft, somewhere off the beaten path, out in the woods, or right here in the middle of this ghost town, danger awaits. We're going to take you way back, drop you right smack dab in the middle of the Old West at its finest. But we're not just going to give you shootouts and bullet wounds and blood splatter. Yes, those things are prominently featured, but there's so much more to this anthology of western horror.

Maybe it's a well-known creature popping in for a visit, or some new creepy crawly monster sucking out your soul, we're going to turn the Old West inside-out and explore its guts to the fullest. There are new adventures to be had, monsters both familiar and unfamiliar to be thwarted… And we're not always going to be the victors. Life in the Old West is hard, trying at its best, and it can wear you down quick.

So, prepare yourself to be transported back in time. Get yourself up on that rickety stagecoach, draw your guns, and let's get going. There's vast territory to cover here, and your journey begins now.

CRIMSON BONES

ed Heather and S.D. Vassallo

23 Gothic tales. Eerie, atmospheric, spooky, and sometimes with a bite. Delve within to satisfy your cravings for darkly tinged stories of love.

Featuring: Valo Wing, Allison Wall, Ariana Ferrante, Devan Barlow, Ariadne Zhou, Desirée M. Niccoli, Agatha Andrews, A. R. Frederiksen, Rebecca E. Treasure, Samantha Lokai, Geraldine Borella, Fatmire Marke, Theresa Tyree, Dana Vickerson, Marianne Halbert, Ann Wuehler, Jessica Peter, Sasha Kielman, Celia Winter, Vivian Kasley, Makeda K. Braithwaite, Samara Auman, H.R. Boldwood, Cindy O'Quinn

A Quaint and Curious Volume of Gothic Tales

ed. Alex Woodroe

A Quaint and Curious Volume of Gothic Tales; 23 stories of madness, pain, ghosts, curses, unspoken secrets, greed, murder, and one of the creepiest collections of dolls ever. Ranging from traditional gothic themes to more modern tropes, this anthology is sure to please the reader…and send a cold shiver or two down their spine.

So, come on in; enter the parlor, find a place by the fire, and experience the beautiful, dark, and occasionally heartbreaking stories told by the authors. The editor, Alex Woodroe, has passionately and carefully curated a powerful volume of stories, written by an amazing and diverse group of contemporary women writers.

WERE TALES: A SHAPESHIFTER ANTHOLOGY

ed S.D. Vassallo and Steven M. Long

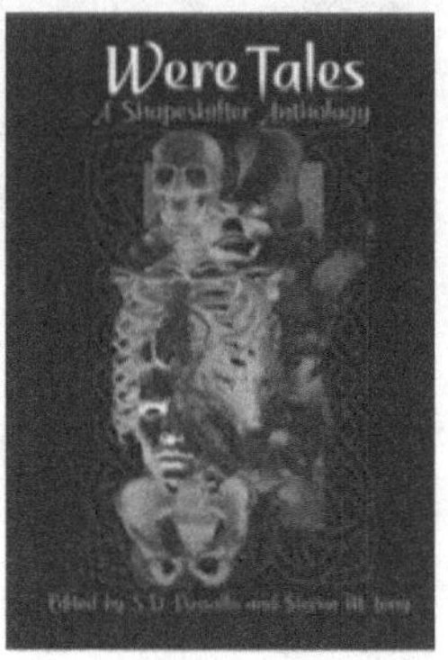

Werewolves. Berserkers. Kitsune. From the most ancient times, tales have been told of people who transform into beasts. Sometimes they're friendly and helpful. Sometimes they're tricksters. And sometimes, they're terrifying.

Were Tales is a collection of scary, thrilling, dark, mysterious, and even humorous short stories and poems of shapeshifters, from the talented minds of Jonathan Maberry, Stephanie Ellis, Gabino Iglesias, Laurel Hightower, Eric J. Guignard, Michelle Garza and Melissa Lason, Shane Douglas Keene, Clara Madrigano, Kev Harrison, Beverley Lee, S.H. Cooper, Elle Turpitt, Catherine McCarthy, Alyson Faye, Theresa Derwin, Ruschelle Dillon, Baba Jide Low, H.R. Boldwood, Ben Monroe, Cynthia Pelayo, Cindy O'Quinn, Sara Tantlinger, Stephanie M. Wytovich, Linda Addison, Villimey Mist, Tabatha Wood, and Christina Sng.

Visit our website at: www.brigidsgatepress.com

www.ingramcontent.com/pod-product-compliance
Lightning Source LLC
Chambersburg PA
CBHW021155310726
48971CB00002B/653